EIGHT
GHOSTS

ENGLISH HERITAGE

EIGHT GHOSTS

The English Heritage Book of
New Ghost Stories

Edited by Rowan Routh

Project concept: Michael Murray-Fennell and Bronwen Riley
Gazetteer: Katherine Davey
Press and publicity: Alexandra Carson
End papers and title page design: Anna Morrison
Typesetter: Ed Pickford

Printed in Poland on paper from responsibly managed,
sustainable sources by Hussar Books

ISBN 978-1-910463-73-4

September Publishing
www.septemberpublishing.org

CONTENTS

'The future is like a dead wall or a thick mist hiding all objects from our view: the past is alive and stirring with objects, bright or solemn, and of unfading interest.'

From 'On the Past and Future' in *Table-Talk; or, Original Essays* by William Hazlitt, 1821

SARAH PERRY

THEY FLEE FROM ME THAT SOMETIME DID ME SEEK

'Did I ever tell you,' said Salma, 'about my friend Elizabeth?'

We sat in the café at Audley End, where we'd come to wheel her mercifully sleeping infant through shaded rooms, and to gaze with due respect at pendant plaster ceilings and extinct waterfowl wading nowhere behind panes of glass.

'Not that I recall.'

'I say friend . . .' Salma paused, and with her right hand rocked the pushchair back and forth. Her face, which habitually had a merry, benevolent look, altered; I saw there, very briefly, an expression of contempt. 'We were never close.'

'You've never mentioned her,' I said.

There was again that contemptuous look, which had in it also a kind of disgust. It troubled me, so that I looked away, and up to where the lawn gave rise to a distant folly.

'She worked here, last year, or perhaps the year before. She's dead now.' This was said with so little expression I had no idea how to respond. 'Look, fetch me coffee, and perhaps some cake, and I'll tell you a story.'

I could hardly complain at the prospect of one of Salma's tales, since she had the gift of contriving an hour's anecdote out of a minute's incident. Dutifully I brought her a steaming pot, and a plate of something sweet. Her child had woken, and was hungry, and she nursed him contentedly; meanwhile the café had begun to fill, so that what she told me then was lost to anyone but me. This was all ten years ago or more: I've not seen Salma since, but the tale has remained with me, like something told to frighten me when I was very young.

Elizabeth (she said) had been one of those charmed and charming folk one would dislike if one could, but never can. She wore old and shabby clothes as though they were velvet and silk; she was a beauty; she had many friends, and her parents seemed to have done her no harm. She'd been a gifted artist as a child, and became a gifted conservator. She'd lived in Paris, restoring a set of opera curtains damaged in a fire, and had once uncovered an art nouveau wall painting concealed behind the plaster of a Norfolk house. Late in the last summer of the last century she was summoned to Audley End. Being an Essex native she was familiar with the house – with its long approach beside a sunny lawn, and its famous yew hedge cut to resemble storm clouds. She was married by then, and if a week's work in her home county lacked the glamour of a Bohemian wall hanging in Prague, it allowed her to stay with her husband in the house where she'd grown up, and with parents to whom she was devoted.

The task for which she was hired was unlike any she'd undertaken before. Wool and silks were her stock-in-trade, and the pads of her fingers were rough with needle-pricks – but at Audley End, she was one of three hired to restore a great Jacobean screen to its former glory. It was carved from oak, and the polish had lost its lustre.

Arriving early at the house – cheerful as ever, if a little nervous – she was greeted at the door.

'Ah! Come along in. Elizabeth, yes? I don't like to contract names. I, for example, am Nicholas, and never Nick – here we are: all is prepared.'

They stood then in the great hall. Banners suspended overhead bore Latin inscriptions; the blinds were lowered. A pair of outlandishly large boots hung above a pale stone staircase that led to a pale stone gallery, and a wasp's nest was concealed in a glass case on a pedestal. It was a warm morning, with a high white haze that promised a scorching day, but nonetheless Elizabeth shivered as she shook the hands of her companions, since a chill rose from the stone floor.

'Morning,' she said, greeting the young men brought bustling forward by Nicholas. 'Ade,' said the first, smiling and shaking her hand. 'And this is Peter, who doesn't speak much.' Peter smiled also, and that smile had in it a kind of wry pleasure that made conversation redundant. Elizabeth felt at once the warm companionship that comes with common purpose.

'Well then,' said Nicholas, proudly, as if he'd carved the screen himself: 'What d'you make of it?'

In truth, Elizabeth's first response was one of distaste. The dark and massy screen ran the breadth of the great hall. At its centre, an arched door was covered in red velvet and flanked by four vast busts that resembled the kings and queens in a deck of cards. It was festooned with carved wreaths, and with wooden bunches of peach, grape and pear, all of which seemed overripe: her eye rested on a pomegranate splitting open to reveal its store of seeds, and she almost thought she caught the scent of rotting fruit. Here and there were other faces: grinning green men and limbless women with hard bulbous breasts. It was all in the Jacobean style, and admirable in its way; but nonetheless she found herself unwilling to meet its many unblinking eyes.

Watching her, Nicholas grinned. 'Odd, isn't it?' he said. Then he drew near, confidingly; it seemed for a moment as if he were about to reveal some secret, but evidently he changed his mind. He clapped his hands together, and briskly rubbed them. 'Not what one would choose for the living room, but well worth a spit and polish. Now then,' he gestured to a trestle table on which cloths, brushes, pots of wax and bottles of solvent were laid out on a white sheet, 'Ade is the expert, I believe? Splendid, splendid. I'll leave you to it, and can be found in the café at lunch.' Departing through the scarlet door he bid a general farewell, though it seemed to Elizabeth he gave her a conspiratorial look as he passed.

The morning went swiftly, with rituals of preparation undertaken in a companionable silence broken only by cautions from Ade, who was an expert in woodwork and had the splinters to prove it. Elizabeth was given charge of a royal pair to the left of the great door, and the pedestals on which they stood. Even from behind the lowered blinds it was possible to feel the heat of the day, which by noon had banished the last of the chill. Her first task was to remove the dust that had settled in the empty eyes of the carved figures, and in the splitting fruit. Her distaste for the screen dissolved as she grew rapt by the grain of the wood and by the skill of the hands that had cut it.

Shortly after noon, by common consent, they left their work. Ade and Peter, having some other appointment, departed in a van, promising to return by close of day. Left alone in the hall it seemed to Elizabeth that the chill had returned: with hands pressed to her aching back she regarded the screen, and the screen regarded her. Then she laughed, and went in search of Nicholas.

It seemed he'd been waiting for her, since the moment she opened the door to the deserted café he beckoned her over.

'How fares it?' he said.

'Well, I think. Although the dust makes me sneeze.'

'I'm sorry you have been abandoned for the afternoon. Will you mind?'

'Not in the least.'

'Splendid! And what do you make of it?'

'Of the screen? It's not to my taste, but it's very fine, isn't it? I found myself thinking: they must have bled over this.'

Her companion did not laugh again, but looked almost comically grave.

'It has a curious history,' he said.

'I should think it does.'

'No, no . . .' He began to fiddle with a button on his cuff. 'Not in the ordinary way. They say it's cursed. Ah, of course you will laugh. Quite right, quite proper.'

'Then you must tell me how, and by whom!'

Seeming both reluctant and delighted, he leaned forward over clasped hands. 'Of course you know the house is built on consecrated land. The first owner had made a pretty penny out of the dissolution of the monasteries, and having turfed out the monks made the abbey his home for a time.'

'The rogue!'

'As it was, so shall it ever be. The abbey already had the very faintest of whiffs about it: one of the monks had hanged himself in the cloister, a sin which is of course unforgivable. It was said he'd been so despised by his brothers that by the end nobody would even meet his eye and Christian forbearance be damned. The loathing simply got too much, I suppose. Wait a moment: aren't you dreadfully hot? – let me bring water.'

He returned with a glass, which she gratefully drank, and resumed his tale. 'The abbey fell into ruin, and the land was passed on; fresh plans were made, new foundations laid; always more wealth, a bigger fireplace, costlier paintings on the walls. The carved screen was a crowning glory of the time: on trend, you might say. Shortly after it was completed one of the workmen killed himself by driving an iron implement into his eye. They say there were other wounds all over his face, as if it had taken several attempts. Nobody attended his funeral.' He looked at her, and there was in his eyes an expression of delight in her discomfort.

'Time passed. Fashion changed, and the screen was painted white – but one of the workmen drank paint and died in agonies fifteen days later, corroded from within.

It's said that neither his wife, nor his children, nor any of his fellow workers, visited him as he lay dying. Again, the fashion changed, and men were hired to scrape the paint from the screen, and restore it to its original form. On the final day one man was missing; they searched, and found him hanging by his belt in the folly up the hill. There was pipe ash scattered about, and the core of an apple: it seemed others had stood by smoking or idly eating, and simply watched him do it.'

Elizabeth was appalled, but didn't like to show it. 'It wouldn't be a proper country house,' she said, 'without a ghost attached.'

'It wouldn't do to say "ghost" precisely: no white sheets here, no grey ladies. The screen does not, I would say, reveal a cowled monk at midnight! It is more – a sensation, if you like. One of desolation, of abandonment – the fear that secretly one is an object of disgust and pity, even to one's family. Haven't we all feared so, in dead of night?'

Elizabeth had always been loved, and always known it; but she nodded, and smiled. 'And it is the screen, they say, that brings about this sensation?'

'So it seems. There have been other incidents – a local woman who came to photograph it was savaged by a gentle dog she'd bottle-fed since birth – but nothing to trouble the makers of vulgar documentaries.'

'Then I'll keep my wits about me!'

'Do so, do so. Well: you'll be hungry, I should think. Don't let me keep you from your cheese-and-tomato.' Straightening his collar in the manner of a man who'd done a good day's work, he left.

A little troubled, Elizabeth gazed for a time at a framed photograph of a Victorian family which hung on the wall. It reflected the summer light, but the glass was uneven, so that it seemed for a moment the wrinkled stockings of a tall girl moved on her bony ankles.

When she had eaten, Elizabeth returned to the great hall. That it had once been so cold as to make her shiver seemed now impossible: particles of dust rose in the hot air. The wax had begun to melt in its pots: there was a sweetish, acrid scent that made her feel drowsy. Left to her own devices she paced the hall: here was the wasps' nest in its case and there the shell of a tortoise emptied of its warm, soft body and hanging hollow on the wall. She imagined it blindly paddling against the wood in a stupid longing to find its living self.

Cursing Nicholas cheerfully for having put her in an eerie frame of mind, she took up her tools and returned to the task. Her head ached, from the heat and from the scent of wax and solvents in the air, and she felt a pulse set up painfully strong in her ears. She thought for a moment of the abbey it once had been – thought of a pale stone cloister, and godly men pacing the paving stones, quietly singing. It called to mind the image of a hanging man, and she wondered vaguely if he'd used his knotted belt, and if perhaps he'd placed the knot against his throat, and that had made things quicker. Out on the lawn a crow croaked; then there was silence, and if it hoped for an answer, there was none.

Seated now beside the screen, Elizabeth felt an irresistible drowsiness come over her. The hollowed tortoise on the wall was still – the wasps in their case were motionless behind the glass – even the dust in the beams of light had ceased to move. Drearily her hand moved across the grinning face of a limbless woman, and it seemed she ought to apologise for so intimate a touch. 'I'm sorry,' said Elizabeth, removing dust from its hollowed eye: 'I'm so sorry.' The pain in her head grew worse, and she leaned for a while upon the screen. The wood was hard, and cool; there came again the croaking crow, and from some distant place a stranger speaking. The heavy air pressed against her and she fell into a doze.

In her sleep it seemed that the screen softened like wax in the heat, and had taken on the pliant soft warmth of skin – seemed she felt it move against her cheek. The air grew still more acrid and more sweet – it was surely the fruit breaking open, the pomegranate blooming mouldy at the split – it was the scent also of flesh, sweating in the evening heat; yes: certainly it was not oak against which she rested but living things, or things not long dead. The limbless woman's torso rose and fell – her grin grew wider – her mouth was not dark but rather crimson, and wet from a passing tongue. 'I am so sorry,' said Elizabeth, suspended between sleeping and waking, uncertain what apology she made, only that it was demanded. Sleepily she reached for the woman, and the woman reached for her – and in the moment before waking she felt against her own mouth the press of another – very soft, very hot; a tender kiss, but one which, with a sensation of abhorrence, woke her at once.

Hours had passed as she dozed – her knees ached from pressure against the stone floor, and the heat had dissipated, leaving behind the old damp chill. For a long moment she could not move: could not bear to look up at the carved woman, with her hard breasts and her smile; and find, perhaps, that there lay now on her lip the tip of a wet tongue. She shook herself from her stupor with laughter at her own absurdity, but all the same could not quite leave the great hall as quickly as she might have liked. It delighted her, then, to see a white van approach as she stood on the threshold of the house: Ade and Peter, returned from their business elsewhere.

'Evening all,' she said, tugging ironically at a forelock. It seemed they didn't recognise her, since there was no return of her cheerful greeting. 'It's me,' she said: 'Elizabeth!'

Ade, at the wheel, would not turn his head; beside him silent Peter looked at her impassively. Then suddenly his face altered, as if a foul smell had reached him: it was faint, but unmistakable – the sneer of a disgusted man. Then the van moved on, and she was left alone. Bewildered, Elizabeth watched them go; and for all the tales she'd been told it merely seemed to her they'd had some business that had gone bad, and put them in a temper. All the same, in the minutes left before her husband came to drive her home, she longed for a moment of something kind and ordinary. She took out her phone, and called her mother.

'Mum?' she said. 'Oh, what a day: what's for dinner, and how have you been?' She waited, but there was no answer. 'Mum?' she said; and then, childish in her anxiety, 'Mummy? Are you there?'

Again, silence; then her mother's voice, but not as she'd ever heard it. It had hardened and acquired edges; it had in it a kind of cool disinterested rage. 'Don't call here,' she said. 'Don't ever call here again.' There was the click of a phone put in its cradle, and in Elizabeth's stomach a moment's roiling terror – then the thought that of course something lay behind it: a bad line, and exasperation with insistent salesmen. Then in the distance – over the bridge and up the pale drive – there came a small car: red, noisy and familiar. Gratefully she ran down the gravel drive, towards the car, picturing everything that was dear about her husband: the hair thinning faintly at the crown, the capable hands on the wheel. Thank God! she thought: thank God!

The car stopped some distance away, and laughing she went on running: how like him, to tease and play – at any moment he'd step out, and run towards her with outstretched arms. But he did not. The sun obscured the windscreen: she could not see his face. Impossible, now, not to forget Nicholas and his tales – the hanging men, the iron-pierced eye – it was all, perhaps, some elaborate unkind joke. She reached the car and rapped against the window, half fond and half impatient. The window did not move. All her cheerful disposition rinsed away, and in its place she felt a kind of panicked dread. She said her husband's name three times; three times he did not reply. At last she knelt, supplicating, beside the car, resting her hands against the door, her face level with the glass: 'Darling?' she said. 'My love?'

He was turned away from her, looking up to the white folly on its low hill. There was the familiar pale brown hair growing over the familiar collar; but something, she knew, had altered. 'Darling?' she said; and slowly – very slowly, as if with the greatest reluctance – he turned. His face, when she saw it, was utterly changed. Gone was the intelligent shy smile, the sudden beam of kindness; in its place was a fixed mask of implacable loathing – very hard, very fixed, as if cut from an unyielding substance. Then it moved, and there was one final flare of hope – that it was all a game; that he would smile, as he'd always smiled. But what came then was a grimace, as if he were looking at some transgression against which every natural human instinct violently rebelled. His hand moved on the wheel – the idling engine stirred – and very quickly, and without looking back, he was gone.

'As I say,' said Salma, lightly stroking her sleeping baby's downy cheek, 'she's dead now. Opened her veins in a warm bath, only not lengthways, as you're supposed to, and it didn't work. In the end she had to break her own head open on the sink. It was a long time before they found her.' The child opened its dusk-blue eyes. He gazed at his mother; she gazed back. It ought to have been delightful to see, but it struck me that Salma was not as lovely looking as I'd always thought: that her eyes were small, and their shine like that of wet stones. 'A very long time,' she said, and I caught a cool, hard note in her voice, which I disliked. 'Nobody looked for her, you see. Nobody wanted her. She wasn't missed.'

ANDREW MICHAEL HURLEY

MR LANYARD'S LAST CASE

I, for one, am thankful of the unwritten statute of decency that compels us not to speak ill of the dead. But perhaps such compassion is driven by a stronger desire to see a man's afflictions and troubles die with him. That way, our own, we hope, might do the same when the time comes.

And so, there was no mention in James Lanyard's obituary this morning of the true circumstances that had led to his withdrawal from public and professional life these past ten years, simply a brief sentence regretting the nervous illness that had overcome him at the Jacobite trials and brought to an end what had been a long and formidable career at the Bar. Some might recall the rumours about what had happened at Carlisle Castle, but only those of us who had been there would know how to separate those rumours from the truth. There was talk of ghosts and spirits (and that Mr Lanyard had in fact been haunted until the day he died in his house on the edge of the Heath) but those are words for a fireside story and inadequate for the real world.

Like most clerks of the Inns, I had heard of James Lanyard well before I met him, and when I began my employment at his chambers his reputation was made flesh exactly. He was commanding in court, with a knowledge of the law that often put his opponent to shame and a noose around the defendant's neck. When there was even the slimmest chance of securing a conviction, he would pursue it with a hound's nose and a terrier's teeth. And even when there wasn't, he forced the gentleman for the defence to work hard for the acquittal.

After the victory at Culloden, it came as no surprise to me that he was selected to represent the Crown when the rebels were tried. He sent nine men to be hanged, drawn and quartered on Kennington Common, and a few weeks later the Earl of Kilmarnock and Lord Balmerino were beheaded at Tower Hill.

There was a desire, that unsettled summer of 1746, for justice to be served quickly in order to stamp down any remaining shoots of rebellion and so, when his duty had been done in London, Mr Lanyard was sent north to prepare for the hearings in Carlisle.

Word had reached us in Lincoln's Inn some weeks earlier that there were already very few lodgings to be had in the city and so I had made arrangements in advance for us to room with Doctor McEwan, an acquaintance of Mr Lanyard's brother, who was a surgeon with the Thirty-Fourth Regiment of Foot. But I had not expected the place to be quite so overrun.

In addition to the rebels captured when the castle fell to the Duke of Cumberland, more prisoners were being sent here from towns on both sides of the border where there was no means of holding them in great numbers or keeping them safe from retribution. And with all these prisoners would come a long procession of lawyers, clerks, underwriters, physicians, men called to the Grand Jury and the Petty Jury, witnesses, families of the accused, bailiffs and a great many other servants and necessaries further down the chain.

The overcrowding was made worse still by the fact that the castle buildings were generally so unfit for use that the soldiers had been garrisoned in the town, together with the French, who, being prisoners of war rather than traitors, were only confined to the city walls. Now and then we'd catch sight of them standing on street corners, bandaged and begging. Some of them looked barely alive.

Even so, said Doctor McEwan that evening at supper, they could count themselves lucky that they were not locked in the dungeons of the keep.

Remembering childhood tales of knights and castles, Perrin, one of Mr Lanyard's junior clerks, imagined that there were chains on the walls and bones in the corners. To which Mr Lanyard bristled and McEwan smiled and cut up bacon rind for his capuchin monkey; payment, he had told us, for once curing a sailor of pox. It was a wrinkled, emaciated creature and clattered about in a small cage with its withered right hand dangling like a bracelet. As soon as we had come into the dining chamber it had started to shriek, and McEwan tried to appease it with scraps off his plate.

The poor animal had been unsettled for months, he said, ever since he had been coming and going from the castle to attend to the prisoners.

'It's the smell of the place, he doesn't like, perhaps,' McEwan suggested. 'I must bring something of the dungeon home with me, I think.'

Then there was the constant noise on the street outside, and it didn't like it when folk came to the door to plead for food. Nor did it tolerate being stared at by strange faces. Or familiar ones, it seemed. For whenever a servant came in, it jumped about as if the cage were being heated from below, and the other junior clerk, Willis, spent the meal looking over his shoulder, half expecting it to break free and leap at him.

'I shouldn't be surprised,' said McEwan, running his thumb over the monkey's forehead as it chewed the nugget of fat in its paw, 'if there were soon no men left in the gaol to try at all.'

'Is it so bad as that?' I said.

'Three hundred men in a room you could pace out in less than two dozen steps, Mr Gregory,' he said, 'I would call it worse than bad.'

'You think traitors deserve better accommodation, doctor?' said Mr Lanyard. 'You think they should be free to wander the streets like the French?'

'Not every man in there will be guilty, Mr Lanyard,' said McEwan. 'You must know that.'

'Not every man in there will be found guilty, I grant you,' Mr Lanyard replied. 'But that's not to say that those who walk free in the end will be innocent.'

'True enough,' said McEwan, 'but all the same, innocent or guilty, I wouldn't have a man die from filth.'

'The brigadier tells me that it has been no more than a dozen,' said Mr Lanyard, nodding when the servant offered him more wine. 'And all of them from injuries sustained in the siege. They are casualties of battle, doctor, not uncleanliness.'

'The brigadier is referring to the dozen that I've been shown,' said McEwan.

'I don't follow your meaning, sir,' said Willis.

'They only want to have the deaths of officers confirmed for their records,' said McEwan. 'The names of the others aren't worth a thing, politically speaking, at least. I don't suppose there's much profit to be made from spreading word that auld Jimmy from the bothy in the glen has expired, is there, Mr Lanyard?'

The capuchin screamed and put its good hand through the bars of the cage, wanting more to eat.

'I am not a politician,' Mr Lanyard replied. 'What use is made of men's names is not my concern. Nor is the condition of the cell from which a man comes to the courtroom. My only responsibility is to try to send him back there.'

'Well, I hope that you never have cause to see the place,' said McEwan, dicing another piece of meat. 'We don't do so well when we're locked up in the dark. Men, I mean. We stumble backwards.'

'They were savages long before they were shut away in the castle,' said Mr Lanyard, and Perrin agreed.

'Savages,' he said.

'Still, I'm sure that they will be glad you've finally come to try them, Mr Lanyard,' said McEwan. 'Then at least, one way or the other, they will be set free.'

He fed some more offcuts through the bars of the cage, but even though the monkey had a handful of food, it chittered and screeched, and Willis knocked his wine across the table.

Doctor McEwan's house was of a modest size and not used to receiving four guests at once. And so while Mr Lanyard had a room of his own, myself, Perrin and Willis were installed in the parlour next to the dining chamber on palliasses. It was cold and cramped and not so tucked away that we couldn't hear the endless clamour from the street outside. But there were plenty of people coming into Carlisle without accommodation at all, and Willis, at least, was simply glad to have a solid door between himself and the doctor's pet, especially when it began to make its noise again in the early hours. It cried and clucked and set the ring grating against the hook of the stand as it flung itself about the cage. It had been disturbed, I assumed, by servants either retiring for the night or starting their morning duties. But if the creature was so prone to making a fuss about being woken, then I thought McEwan would surely have forbidden any of his staff from taking short cuts through the dining chamber after hours. Only, it screamed for much longer than it would have taken someone merely to pass by. It seemed to me that someone was standing there and watching it and having fun stoking its temper.

✦

The days that followed were all spent at the castle, sifting through the many volumes of evidence for the Grand Jury to decide which of the three hundred or so prisoners would be put before the judges. Some were too sick to be tried, some died before a decision was made about them and others were clearly simpletons with little understanding of what they had been fighting for in the first place. Mr Lanyard was reluctant to agree to the scheme, but to reduce the numbers further the judges ordered that prisoners from the common ranks draw lots in order to determine which of them would be put on trial and which would be transported.

Now and then, I saw men being brought out of the keep in chains to be loaded onto wagons. Men of a kind at least. Hair and bones. As decrepit as the buildings of the courtyard.

During the siege the previous winter, Cumberland had called the castle an old hen coop, and even though it might have been a means of making the task in hand seem less daunting to his men, it wasn't so far off the mark. His artillery had ruptured walls that had been falling apart for a long time.

The dreariness of the place was made worse by the weather too. It was only the beginning of August, but the autumn had come early to this part of the country and the drizzle that swept over the castle seemed to loosen all colour from the walls. The sandstone dripped in various reds and browns, like a paint palette up-ended and left to ooze itself clean.

In the old palace where we, the prosecution, had been given a room to work, the windows ran with condensation even though the fires were lit, and I expected Mr Lanyard's health to suffer. In the courtroom he always presented himself as a man with a physical strength to match that of his intellect, but privately – his robes on the peg and his wig on the stand – he complained of a number of ailments. Cold, damp weather exacerbated his lumbago and for years he had smarted from an ulcerated stomach.

Which may be the reason – I console myself – that I did not think too much of his hunched appearance during those weeks he spent at the table poring over the masses of paper. It simply wasn't uncommon to see him in discomfort and, despite McEwan's offers of salts and liniments, he relieved the aches in his usual way, with a half bottle of claret at supper. He did not speak very much either, but then, like myself, Perrin and Willis, he was tasked with reading reports and witness statements and letters and petitions that were so numerous and complex that it was several weeks before their contents had been examined to any kind of satisfaction.

No, it wasn't until the trials began in the second week of September that I noticed anything odd about his behaviour at all.

The first two days of hearings were successful and he managed to suppress his pains well enough to secure a good number of convictions. He was eloquent and shrewd in his questioning, and the judges commended him on his preparations. But during adjournments he was on edge and developed the habit of brushing the back of his hand, as though a spider had crawled across it. He was nauseous too and frequently called the servants to bring more water. It was the smell of the courtroom, perhaps, that affected him.

The prisoners were given a cursory sousing in the yard outside before they were presented to the judges, but this only served to make them seem more wretched in a way. Their beards dripped like the matted tails of hill-sheep, they bled from sores that would not heal, and despite the bucket of water that the soldiers had thrown at each of them, they were still soiled to the knees as if they had emerged from a sewer. The odour became so strong in the afternoons that one of the judges, Mr Clark, ordered that after every third hearing the floor be swept. With fresh straw laid down and the benches strewn with rosemary, the air was improved considerably, and yet it seemed to make no difference to Mr Lanyard. He sweated and swallowed and could hardly get through his questions without his voice deteriorating into a coughing fit.

Twice Mr Clark asked if he wished to adjourn, but Mr Lanyard insisted on continuing until the end of the session, by which time half of the twenty-two men on trial that day had been convicted. Though, I have to say that it was due to the overwhelming evidence against them more than any skill of examination or discovery on Mr Lanyard's part. All afternoon, he had struggled to speak and when he was seated to hear the defence he settled and resettled his bulk on the chair and pressed his handkerchief to his nose so often that it began to seem like some tactic of distraction.

Even when we returned to Doctor McEwan's house in the evening he was no better and would not eat for fear that he would see his supper on his shoes. McEwan advised him to take some mint leaves from the garden but the mere thought of letting anything past his lips made Mr Lanyard pale and he complained again about the smell of the men in the courtroom. How it lingered on his clothes.

'The capuchin smells it too,' he said as the animal rattled its cage.

Perhaps it could. It seemed to have taken a particular dislike to Mr Lanyard and bared its pin teeth and hissed in its throat until McEwan finally ordered it to be taken out of the dining chamber.

The next two days passed in much the same way and Mr Lanyard slept poorly and barely ate. In court, when he was waiting for the defence to finish, I saw him inspecting his reflection in the water jug, peering at his left shoulder and then as discreetly as possible turning to look behind him as if there were someone there.

The sixth day of the trials proved to be Mr Lanyard's last. After that he could do no more and did not set foot in a courtroom again.

His final case was that of a man called Fraser, captured when the castle fell. Like many of the Scottish prisoners, he spoke little English, and so the procedure was doubled in length while questions and answers were passed back and forth through the translator.

His case was like so many others that we'd heard day after day. Being a clansman, his chief had ordered him to fight and because he had been ordered to fight he could not refuse. If he had, then his cattle would have been taken from him and his house torn down. It was a claim corroborated by the witness for the Defence, who had seen Mr Fraser pressed into service in the most brutal manner, but refuted by two other men captured after the siege and turned King's evidence.

The first, from the Cameron clan, said that he knew Fraser well and that he had seen the man leading troops at the Battle of Falkirk. The second, of the clan Gordon, matched the statement and added that he had been garrisoned with Fraser at Carlisle to hold up Cumberland as he pursued the Young Pretender's army north. He swore on the life of King George that what he said was true and when Mr Lanyard, dabbing his brow with a handkerchief, put this to him, the prisoner answered, '*Tha e coma mu Rìgh Deòrsa.*'

'He says that the witness cares nothing for King George,' the translator said.

'No?' said Mr Lanyard, coughing into his fist. 'Then why does he give evidence against you?'

The translator asked Fraser the question, who replied, '*B' fhearr leis gu robh mi marbh.*'

'He says that Mr Gordon wants him dead, sir,' the translator explained.

'Then Mr Gordon must be assured of your guilt,' said Mr Lanyard.

'Pardon me, sir,' the translator said, 'the defendant says that Mr Gordon wants him dead, but not for treason.'

'You have committed some other crime?' said Mr Lanyard.

Fraser said that he had not, but that Mr Gordon thought so.

Mr Lanyard frowned and said, 'He thinks so? What crime does he accuse you of?' and as the question was being put to Fraser by the translator, Mr Lanyard jerked his hand as though he had been touched. He looked behind him, looked down, in fact.

'Is there something troubling you, Mr Lanyard?' asked Mr Clark.

Mr Lanyard touched his fingers and stared at the bare floorboards.

'No, my lord,' he said.

'Do you have anything else to ask the defendant?' said Mr Clark.

Mr Lanyard wiped his brow with the sleeve of his robe. 'Might I request that the floor is cleared, my lord?' he said. 'The smell is stifling.'

'The floor will be swept at the end of the session, Mr Lanyard,' said Mr Clark. 'If you are unwell, then I shall adjourn.'

'A moment, my lord,' said Mr Lanyard and sat down heavily in his chair and drank the cup of water I poured for him. But he had taken no more than a mouthful before he jerked his arm as if he had been squeezed on the elbow and soaked the papers in front of him.

'What is it, Mr Lanyard?' I asked, but he was looking behind his chair.

Voices began to murmur around the room and Mr Clark struck his gavel on the block.

'Mr Lanyard,' he said. 'I ask again. Are you unwell, sir?'

'Who is it?' said Mr Lanyard. 'There is someone here. My hand.'

He held it at arm's length, as though it did not belong to him. His palm and his fingers dripped with the same slurry that coated Fraser's shins.

The defendant and the witnesses looked at one another and the noise in the courtroom increased enough for Mr Clark to sound his gavel a second time.

Mr Lanyard twitched again and now his other hand was soiled.

'What is this trickery?' he said and started from his chair as quickly as his body would allow, his eyes moving as though he was watching the progress of a wasp around the courtroom. He let out a cry and crouched by one of the windows with his hands over his ears as if some loud, piercing noise had suddenly erupted.

Every man in the courtroom was on his feet now, Mr Clark's demands for silence having no effect. Fraser, Cameron and Gordon argued as the bailiffs kept them separated. And through it all Mr Lanyard sobbed like a child, and was still curled up, mired in his robes, when the courtroom had been cleared and Doctor McEwan arrived.

Back at McEwan's house, Mr Lanyard still seemed agitated, and even with his clothes taken off to be washed and in a clean nightshirt he insisted that he could still smell the dungeon. And blood too. As if it were a vapour in the room.

McEwan called the servants to fill the copper bath and urged Mr Lanyard to try and scrub the stench from his skin. Though it was doubtful he was listening. His mind was as unsettled as his eyes, which roved from one corner to the next.

'There is someone here,' he said, 'as there was in the courtroom.'

'It is only Mr Gregory and I,' said McEwan. 'No one else.'

'There is another,' said Mr Lanyard.

'Try to sleep, sir,' said McEwan. 'And in the morning you will find yourself much relieved of these thoughts, I'm sure.'

We left him to rest and went down to eat, although none of us were hungry. Perrin and Willis barely touched their food and went out into the garden for some air.

'He will be well again,' McEwan said. 'I'm sure he will regain his vigour.'

But I knew that they were words of reassurance only and that he could not imagine Mr Lanyard being able to continue. The man was utterly exhausted in his body and in his mind.

McEwan was turning in for the night and halfway up the stairs when we heard Mr Lanyard calling for us and the capuchin screeching. It had got loose from its cage.

The doctor was first to reach the room and I and the two servants followed, finding the animal clinging to Mr Lanyard's back. Each time we tried to get hold of its arm or leg or tail, it would dart out of reach and fix its claws in a different bit of flesh, causing Mr Lanyard to cry out in pain. His nightshirt was already torn and spotted with blood and his unwigged scalp raked with scratches.

I suppose it was the noise of Perrin and Willis coming into the room that finally drove the creature to leap down onto the floor and make for the open door. But before it could escape, Perrin threw a blanket over it and then he and Willis and the servants stamped until it was dead.

While the bundle was removed, McEwan attended to Mr Lanyard's wounds, making all efforts to keep his hands steady. When he had finished, I took him down into the dining chamber and sent a servant to fetch him some brandy. McEwan looked overcome with remorse but I assured him that he was not at fault. Animals were animals. They knew no better. He replied that he could not blame the two clerks for wishing to defend their master, and that the creature could not have been allowed to run wild in the house, but the capuchin had not meant to attack Mr Lanyard as he slept. It had been drawn there to see off someone else.

'An intruder?' I said.

'You may call it that,' replied McEwan and drank his brandy and said no more.

It wasn't until some months later, when the trials were over and Mr Lanyard's replacement had sent dozens more men to swing on the forthcoming market days, that Doctor McEwan wrote to properly express his regret, not only about what had happened but for the lurid rumours that had begun to attach themselves to my old employer. Time had allowed his thoughts to settle and, on the proviso that I shared it with no one else, he offered his account of what he had seen in Mr Lanyard's room, what he suspected the capuchin had been frightened of that night and for many months before. He had only seen it for a moment before the sheets were disturbed by the frenzy of the animal's assault, but there had been someone lying next to Mr Lanyard. He could swear to that, even if he could not be sure who it was.

It at least looked like the boy he'd seen pulled out of the dungeon one night in the winter. A pale sheaf of bones. No more than eleven or twelve. Recruited with his father, who had been killed in the siege.

McEwan said that the soldier who had called him into the keep knew that he ought to have disposed of the child, but compassion had got the better of him and he wanted the doctor to at least confirm that he was dead. And he was, McEwan wrote. He had been for days. But not from some sickness brought on by the noxious air in the dungeon or the fetid pool that was knee deep with what the men had excreted day after day.

The guard had told him that at the very back of the cell there was some opening through which rainwater trickled, and that the men would take it in turns to lick the stones. It seemed that this boy had spent too long at the wall and in the dark the others had broken his skull, and then drowned him.

MARK HADDON

THE BUNKER

Nadine was returning from a day shift at the hospital when it happened for the first time. A fug of sweat and cigarettes and damp coats on the top deck of a No. 23, then a windy walk high over the river on that fine white rainbow of cast iron, stopping at the central point, as she always did, to lean over the railings and pretend for a few moments that she was airborne like the ravens that played out there in the updraught.

Past the laundrette, the bookies and The Trawlerman, then dipping into the Co-operative for a *Telegraph* and the pint of milk her mother-in-law would almost certainly have forgotten to buy.

She crossed the cool, tiled hall of The Mansions and stepped into the lift. A ring of light appeared around her fingertip as she pressed the button for the fifth floor. The doors closed, the slack in the cable was taken up and she rose through the building.

Halfway between the second and third floors she tasted something bitter at the back of her throat. Her legs became unsteady and she had to grip the metal rail to hold herself upright. The brushed steel of the lift's wall, the emergency sign, her own hands, none of them seemed real. There was a loud, sparking crackle and the world shrank to a single bright point, like a television screen being turned off. She floated briefly in absolute darkness, then light and noise flooded back and she was standing, not in the lift, but at the side of a busy road looking at a row of dirty red-brick houses in the rain. The street was full of people, running, shouting, crying. One woman simply stood and stared into the distance, one dropped bags of shopping at her feet, a tin of Ambrosia creamed rice rolling into the gutter through spilt flour turning milky on the wet pavement.

A white and sky-blue panda car screeched to a halt at the kerb beside her and a policeman got out. 'Nadine Pullman?'

She was too shocked to reply, shocked that she was visible, shocked that someone knew her name, that she was not just looking at this scene but a part of it.

'Get in.' She didn't move. 'I'm serving you with a B 47 notice, now sodding get into the car or I swear by Almighty God . . .'

She got into the car. The policeman jumped back into the driving seat and gunned the engine. A woman in an olive gaberdine grabbed the wing mirror and screamed for help. They roared away from the kerb and she tumbled backwards, holding the ripped-off mirror in her hands.

The car tilted and squealed round the corners. A zigzagging Bedford truck came close to hitting them.

'What's happening?' It was her voice but it wasn't her voice.

'What the bloody hell do you think is happening?'

They crested a hill and skidded into a small lane. 'Out!' He left the key in the ignition. Three men were running up a concrete staircase built into a high grass bank. One of them was wearing a butcher's apron. She could hear sirens. 'Move!' She tripped and lost a shoe. The policeman grabbed her arm and dragged her up the steps, scraping her ankles and ripping her stockings. He pulled her through a thick double door into a crowded entryway then let her drop. A man and a woman ran up the steps behind them waving cream certificates with red seals.

A bald man in spectacles barked, 'Last two!' and as they crossed the threshold he swung the heavy door shut and it rang like a gong. He locked it with quarter-turns of the levers at its four corners.

There was another sparking crackle, everything shrank to a similar bright point, and after a few seconds of darkness Nadine found herself lying on the floor of the lift. How long had she been away? Seconds? Minutes? The door was open and Mr Kentridge, from flat seventeen was staring down at her. 'Are you unwell, Mrs Pullman?'

She got slowly to her feet, explaining that it was her time of the month and that this sometimes made her sick and light-headed. 'I need to go and sit down.'

He held up his hands, not wanting to continue a conversation on this subject. She walked to the door of the flat, steadying herself against the wall then turned to make sure that he had entered the lift and descended.

Martin's mother was asleep on the yellow sofa, eyes closed, head resting against the antimacassar. Bennie was dozing in her lap, thumb in his mouth. She wanted a cup of tea but didn't trust her shaking hands with the kettle, the matches and the gas. Instead she opened the window and lit a Kensitas. The sun was starting to go down and lights were coming on, the dark buildings turning slowly into advent calendars.

The panic in the streets, the green metal door, the airlock. There was no doubt about it. Mr Kentridge suspected nothing, that was some consolation. She massaged her forehead as if the problem were nothing more than a headache. From miles away she heard the sad song of a ferry clearing the harbour. That unforgettable vision of her uncle's final minutes, so clear she forgot sometimes that she had not witnessed them with her own eyes, the neighbours dragging him out of the cottage and into the little strip of woodland beside the railway. She had seen him a couple of days before the end, raving about sinks and fire orders and black holes. Her aunt's desperate desire to save him warring with the knowledge that the fight was already lost. 'There's nothing more that we can do, Nadine. Please. We need to get away from here.' Hoping that the doctors would reach him first. Though who knew which fate was worse.

'Mummy . . .?' Bennie was waking.

They said that if you'd been there once then you were lost. Though who would be foolish enough to broadcast their good luck if they had visited the other world and come back merely scorched?

'Mummy . . .?'

She cooked a lamb and carrot stew. She remembered and forgot and remembered, every occasion a jug of iced water down her spine. Edith complained about her hip. She heard herself being sympathetic and was surprised at the skill with which she dissembled. Bennie was teething. She rubbed clove oil on his gums. What would happen to him? Not just the absence of a mother but the taint of having had this mother in particular.

Martin returned just after seven. Nadine hoped he would sense her distress but he was preoccupied with some difficulty at the workshop involving a three-piece suite and an unpaid bill. After supper he played cribbage with his mother and piggybacks with Bennie then put him to bed. The three of them listened to Joan Sutherland on the radio.

She lay under the covers unable to sleep, Martin dead to the world beside her. So gentle for such a big man. She'd seen him lift a car so that the wheel could be changed. They'd met at a coffee concert in the Wellesley Room, Martin absurd in his undersized suit. Haydn's 'Sunrise' before the interval, Beethoven's *Grosse Fuge* after. Two brilliant violins poorly served. He could protect her. She had thought it before they'd even spoken.

She had two fathers. One was sober, one was drunk. The first became the second when the sun went down. The beatings weren't the worst. It was the waiting in between which ate away at her. She brought Martin home for tea and Martin held her father's eye for the most uncomfortable ten seconds of her life and her father never touched her again. But now? This wasn't a drunken father. This wasn't a flat tyre and a missing jack.

Above her in the gloom the plaster cornices turned slowly monstrous.

Three uneventful days encouraged the hope that she'd had a very narrow escape, the burden of her terrible secret growing slowly lighter as she changed dressings and emptied bedpans. The man who had fallen from the scaffolding two months earlier took his first steps and they threw a party.

On the fourth day she was sitting on one of the benches outside the staff canteen, next to the blackthorn hedge which half-hid the boiler plant. She was eating the mustard and potted meat sandwich she had made that morning and wrapped in greaseproof paper so that she could carry it in her handbag. Again, the bitter taste, the sparking crackle, the darkness and suddenly she was holding an exercise book bearing a black crown and the words 'AWDREY LOG: Supplied for the Public Service HMSO Code 28-616'. She could smell sweat and human excrement. Mounted on the wall to her right was a grid of tiny wooden boxes, the kind a school librarian might use for storing index cards. One was labelled 'DEAD', another 'CONFIRMED'.

Three men in pigeon-blue military jackets were leaning over a broad table. Behind them was a wall of Perspex on which a big map of the country had been gridded and sub-divided. She was in a room not much larger than a squash court. It had no windows. One of the men looked up. His stubble and his red eyes suggested that he had neither slept nor shaved for several days. 'Well . . .?'

'Two new blasts. Blast one: 50 miles, bearing 152 degrees.' The words were coming out of her mouth but she had no idea what they meant. '6 to 8 megatons. RAF Scampton.'

'Dear God,' said the man. 'And the second blast . . .?'

'The second . . .' Her mind was blank.

'For Christ's sake, we do not have all day.'

His colleague turned to him, a gangly man with a wizard's beard who was clearly not used to wearing a uniform. 'I fear that we have all the time in the world.'

'Miss Pullman.' The red-eyed man turned back to Nadine.

'A little kindness would not go amiss,' said the bearded man.

'Miss Pullman,' the red-eyed man ignored his colleague, 'there is limited air. There is limited water. You have a job to do and that is the only reason you are here. Illness is not an option. Mental collapse is not an option.'

The sparking crackle sounded again and after a short period of darkness she was lying on her back staring up at a blue sky, the blackthorn bush and two worried people gazing down at her. Dr Cairns offered a hand to ease her to her feet. Sister Collins guided her to the bench. Cold sweat and a deep churn in her guts. 'Nurse Catterick, fetch Nurse Pullman a glass of cold water.'

It was simply a matter of time now. Her friends and colleagues wouldn't turn her in, but gossip spread and it only took one person who valued their safety above your life. Dr Peterson had been taken away in a black van, Nurse Nimitz had been taken away, the handsome Trinidadian man with sickle cell had been taken away . . .

She went home early, bright autumn sun falling on a world to which she no longer belonged. There was a fair in Queen's Gardens, a chained baby elephant in a nest of straw, painted horses turning, a jaunty pipe organ and the smell of burnt sugar.

She had no idea what to expect from this point on. They had wiped her uncle from the family record, as if ignorance were a form of protection, and what she heard elsewhere was a tangle of gossip, half-truth and scaremongering. Some said that it was contagious insanity, others that these were echoes of past events, others that they were premonitions of events still to come. The end of the world, some whispered.

There were no articles in the papers. It was not discussed on the radio or the television. Her lack of interest seemed shameful in retrospect. Not once had she put herself in these shoes. So much suffering and her only thought had been relief that it was happening to someone else.

She had Bennie on her knee when it happened for a third time. *This is the way the ladies ride. Clip-clop, clip-clop . . .*

Edith had retreated to her room with *The Grand Sophy* and a mug of cocoa which might or might not have contained a shot of Bowmore, and Bennie was hungry for some of the riotousness that Edith's age and hip were making increasingly impossible. *This is the way the gentlemen ride . . .*

It was quicker this time, more like a doorway than a journey. No bitter taste, just a rapid crackle, Bennie falling backwards out of her grasp, then she was waking from a shallow sleep in a cramped dormitory of eight bunks. Half-submarine, half-boarding school. Her skin was sticky, her hair lank. A woman in uniform was waiting to take her place under the dirty sheet and khaki blanket. The words 'Royal Observer Corps' curved over a red aeroplane on her shoulder. Nadine looked down and saw that she had been sleeping in an identical grey-blue uniform. Fifteen other women were climbing out of bed. Fifteen different women were waiting to take their places.

Someone was singing. 'I never knew I'd miss you . . . Now I know what I must do . . . Walking back to happiness . . . I shared with you.'

'For God's sake, Rita. Can it, will you.'

'Girls, girls . . .'

The women crossed the corridor and entered the room she recognised from the last time. The strip lights, the

Perspex wall-maps. She was the tail of the crocodile. The red-eyed man stepped in front of her and closed the door so that they were alone in the corridor. The chug of machinery somewhere and the faint odour of diesel fumes. She could see now that there was a triangle of waxy flesh on his chin where no stubble grew. He had been burnt as a child, perhaps.

'I need to know one thing and one thing only.'

'What's that?'

'Can you do your job?'

She closed her eyes and looked into her mind and saw fragments of something which had broken or fallen apart . . . a boiler suit made of white cotton . . . the EM wave and the optical wave . . . the sound of someone weeping at the end of a phone line . . .

'Miss Pullman . . . ?'

She felt a rising panic and a painful yearning to be somewhere safe with no responsibilities. She began to sob.

'I think that's a fairly conclusive "no".'

Martin sat in the rocking chair beside the bed. She had been away for longer this time.

'Where's Bennie . . . ?'

'He bumped his head. My mother has taken him to the fair. Toffee apple and candy floss. Then he can go on the merry-go-round and be royally sick.'

'I should have told you, earlier.'

He cupped her cheek in his hands and shook his head. Was he saying goodbye? Were the doctors drumming their fingers in the living room, giving the two of them a final few moments' grace? Under the fear was a relief she had not expected.

'We're going to see an exorcist.'

Were it not for the steady confidence of his gaze she might have questioned his sanity. She had heard about exorcists only in third- and fourth-hand stories. She had always assumed that they were figments of desperate imaginations.

'There are things I have never told you.' He got to his feet. 'Things you were safer not knowing.' He handed her the black duffel coat he had laid over the arm of the chair. 'Put this on. We have a long, cold walk ahead of us.'

They slipped into an alleyway off Weaver's Lane. They cut across the graveyard of St Saviour's. Martin was a big man who attracted attention but the few people who passed them in the darkened streets took little notice. Only a dog was disturbed by their presence, growling at the end of its chain, hackles up and head down. It was the strangeness of the evening perhaps, or her growing detachment from her own life, but she felt as if she were traversing a city which was almost but not quite identical to the one in which she lived.

He said, 'I told you sometimes that I would be working late. It was not always true.' He said, 'I've never talked about my sister. We lost her. I promised I would never lose anyone again.' He said, 'I've done this for nineteen other people. I hoped I'd never have to do it for you.'

They were heading downhill towards the docks. Fish and marine oil on the wind. The lights of The Raleigh still blazed, its patrons blurry behind dripping, foggy glass. They walked through a mazy canyon of warehouses. A big rat trotted casually past like a tiny insurance clerk late for the office. A precise half-moon lit their way.

They turned a corner and the moon was swallowed by a double-funnelled steamer in red and cream, roped to the quayside and port-holed on three decks from stem to stern.

Martin led her to the foot of a cast-iron fire escape which rose steeply to a door between two dirty, lit windows which might have been the eyes of a harbourmaster's office were it not for the lack of signage. They mounted the ringing steps.

The exorcist was a plump, forgettable woman whose ivy-green cardigan was fastened by walnut-brown toggles. She greeted Martin with the wordless nod one gave to a colleague. 'So this is Nadine.'

There was a Rolodex. There was a vase of dying irises. There was a framed reproduction of Bruegel's *Fall of Icarus*, cracked at the corner. A bagatelle board leaning against a wall would have seemed bizarre on any other day. Nadine took the empty armchair.

'I'm afraid we have no time for pleasantries.' The woman was steelier than she appeared. 'You have to trust me completely and you must do exactly as I say. There is no alternative.' Nadine glanced round and Martin nodded his assent. 'The next time you cross over I will be waiting for you on the other side. We will not mention this meeting. We will not talk of Martin or your son. We will not talk of this world. Do you understand?' The woman leant forwards and Nadine saw a charm bracelet slip from the cuff of her cardigan, a silver chain from which hung a little silver crow, a little silver moon and a little silver hammer.

'I understand.'

'I will try hard to find you a way home. I cannot tell you in advance what it will be. I can only tell you that I have not failed yet.' Somewhere nearby the bell of a mariner's chapel tolled twice. 'I must go. I have difficult work to do.' The exorcist stood slowly. She seemed to be in some pain. 'When you next see me I will be changed.'

She took a macramé shoulder bag and a dark blue cagoule from the back of the chair. 'Get some rest.' Then she was gone.

Martin sat on the arm of the chair and held Nadine. She had many questions, but to ask any of them would open the door of the aircraft mid-flight. Better not to see how far she had to fall. She wanted more than anything to be with Bennie.

'Remember that first long walk we took?' Martin sandwiched her tiny hand between his great paws. 'Near Minehead?' A thundercloud had risen over Selworthy Beacon and the sunshine was replaced suddenly by a slate sky and hail like conkers. They ran hand in hand for a pillbox where they startled the sleeping, ownerless spaniel who would later accompany them for the remainder of the walk. 'Let's take it again . . .'

She leant her head against the dependable mass of him. 'OK.'

'So . . . I picked you up from your parents' house. It was half-past nine in the morning. You were wearing the orange skirt with the yellow circles . . .'

An hour, two hours . . . She slept and woke and did not recognise her surroundings and was briefly terrified until she saw Martin, only to succumb to a different fear when she remembered why she was here with the dying irises and the bagatelle board. She slept again and woke and drank a glass of tepid water from the pitcher on the desk and was standing at the window watching faint smudges of peach light pick out the cranes and the hulks at anchor when she left the world for the final time.

No taste, no noise, no darkness. Instantly she was sitting at a Formica-topped table in a canteen. On the far side of the table was the gangly, bearded man. Behind him sat a uniformed woman Nadine did not recognise. She had a lazy eye and black, black hair. There was a serving hatch and the rank perfume of boiled vegetables. She looked around for the exorcist but there was no one else in the room. The Formica had unglued itself from the chipboard at the table's corner.

'I apologise for Major Pine's graceless behaviour. He is correct, but there are many different ways of being correct.' She could hear now that the man's accent was a soft, lowland Scots. 'In better times you would have been cared for.' He sighed. 'But in better times our lives would not depend on a man like Major Pine.'

His female colleague sat back and said nothing, as if she were supervising the man's training.

He cleared his throat and read from the sheaf of stapled papers. 'You signed documents during your training to the effect that if, on active service with ROC No. 20 Group, you became incapacitated either physically or mentally . . .' He dropped the paper '. . . and some more turgid bureaucratic nonsense I won't bore you with.' He rubbed his eyes.

'They want you to sign a form. Can you believe that? Because the last man in the world will be some prig from Whitehall trudging across the scorched wasteland checking paperwork.' The woman seemed neither surprised nor affronted by the diatribe. He pushed a pamphlet across the table. 'Predictably, they provide a helpful guide to the situation.'

Expulsion: Instructions for Short Term Survival. She flipped through the pages. 'Root vegetables from allotments and gardens may provide another source of relatively uncontaminated food . . .' There was a diagram showing how to kill a poorly drawn dog, though whether for protection or consumption it was not immediately clear. She was transfixed by the backs of the hands that were and weren't hers, the dirt under the nails, the faint blue of returning blood. They were so real. She had never heard anyone speak about how utterly convincing it all was.

'You know as much as anyone.' The man shrugged. 'Leeds has gone. Manchester has gone. The destruction is widespread from Holy Loch south. In other circumstances I would pray for God to go with you, but my faith in the old chap has been somewhat undermined of late.' He stood up and pushed his chair back under the table, the legs screeching on the lino. 'I wish you a strong wind off the North Sea and a cache of tinned beans.' He gestured towards the door. 'Let's get this ghastly business over with.'

The woman followed them into the corridor. Where was the exorcist? Nadine was increasingly certain that something had gone wrong. The man stood aside so that she could take the stairs first. Nadine felt sick. None of this was real. She had to remember that.

The man waited for a few seconds then said, 'I would much rather that this passed off without any unpleasantness.'

She climbed to the concrete landing where she had entered the building that first time. A big cream hatch stood open revealing an airlock not much larger than a toilet cubicle. Rubber seals, pressure gauges and a red warning light in a sturdy wire cage. The far wall was a sealed, identical hatch. And beyond that?

'It will be cold outside.' The black-haired woman held out a black duffel coat, identical to the one Nadine had worn for the long walk earlier that evening, but older and dirtier with a skirl of torn lining dangling below the hem. Worlds slid over one another, like a cathedral in a café window, like the beach and the christening on the same photograph.

And then she saw them, in the shadow of the woman's military cuff, a crow, a moon, a hammer. 'Thank you.'

The man stared hard at the wall over Nadine's shoulder, unwilling to meet her eye. She stepped into the airlock. She was not going to turn round. She was not going to treat him like a real person. She focused instead on a long cream-coloured drip where a painter had over-loaded his brush. Were these the echoes of some vanished world? Was this the future? It seemed inconceivable that her own mind could conjure a universe so rich in detail.

The man said, 'I wish you luck,' the hinges squeaked and, with a soft kiss, seal met seal. There were four muffled clangs as the locks were turned on the landing then nothing, only the sound of her breathing in the steel chamber.

She closed her eyes and pictured herself unconscious in the armchair in that little room, Martin at the window waiting for her to be returned to him. Outside, dockers yelled and busy tugboats worked at the jigsaw puzzle of the big freighters. Bananas and coal and coffee. Bennie would surely be awake now, wanting to know where she was.

Nadine opened her eyes. There was a dirty grille at waist height. There was an abandoned pair of black wellington boots. There was a waste bin bearing the label 'Contaminated Overalls Only'. In what way was a duffel coat meant to help? Had she deceived herself? Had she seen what she wanted to see in the glitter of some other jewellery?

The red light came on and began to turn. Then the alarm went off, stupidly loud for such a small space. She covered her ears. Five, six seconds? The alarm stopped and the light went out. She took her hands from her ears and heard the dull hiss of air pressures equalising. The big door unlocked itself and let in a thin slice of grey light and a sweet, charred smell which raised the hairs on the back of her neck. She put the duffel coat on for the small comfort it offered and carefully opened the door.

The panda car was burnt out, the paint black and blistered. Orange rust was already eating away at the unprotected metal, the tyres were gone, the glass was gone. There were no windows in any of the buildings. Many walls had fallen. Roofs were shipwrecks of black timbers. A thick, unwashed fog hid the far side of the park across the road. Every patch of grass was dead. She walked down the steps. Two silhouettes on a nearby wall looked like the shadows of children if children could leave shadows behind. The airlock bumped softly shut behind her. She listened. It was the kind of silence she had only ever heard on a still day in the mountains.

A burnt dog lay beside the burnt car.

There was movement in the corner of her eye. She turned and saw a tramp standing at the lane's dead end, holding the hand of a girl of seven or eight. Their faces were soiled. He wore three dirty coats and carried a crowbar. There was an open wound on the girl's cheek.

'Oi! Lady!'

The woman had been right. The air was bitterly cold.

She slipped her hands into the pockets of the duffel coat. There was something hard and heavy in the right-hand side. She lifted out a tarnished, snub-nosed pistol. The words 'Webley & Scott Ltd, London & Birmingham' were stamped into the side of a fat, square stock. The trigger guard was a primitive hoop and the hammer looked like a sardine key. A gentle squeeze of the trigger showed that the machinery was oiled and ready.

'You were in that bloody bunker, weren't you!' The man was limping towards her, dragging the girl behind him. 'You did this!' He swung the crowbar around, indicating the fallen walls, the dead grass. 'You people did this!'

Suddenly she understood. *You have to trust me completely.* Nothing had gone wrong. The exorcist had found her a way home.

'Are you listening to me, lady?'

She put the barrel of the gun into her mouth and bit the metal hard to hold it steady.

KAMILA SHAMSIE

FOREBODING

'I don't believe in ghosts,' Khalid said, his first day on the job as a security guard at Kenilworth Castle.

'Neither do I,' said the gardener, who had stopped at the staff kitchen for a cup of tea. 'But when something funny happens that you can't explain, just remember the ghosts here aren't malicious. The boys on the top floor are mischievous – forever moving things around. And him along the corridor doesn't like people in his space but he only gets a bit shouty. Or so I've heard from those who can actually see him. But there's no harm involved.'

'I'd stay away from the mere at night though,' said the property supervisor, handing around a packet of digestives. 'There was that siege in 1266; bodies catapulted over the walls, starvation, disease. If there really are ghosts of soldiers in the mere, they won't be happy.'

'What do ghosts do when they're unhappy?' Khalid asked, trying not to let any of what he was thinking enter his tone of voice. *When you've lived through wars you don't need to invent stories to scare you. Memory is more frightening than imagination.*

'I don't know. I stay away from the mere at night,' the property supervisor said, with a big laugh that made it acceptable to believe or not believe, just so long as you did it in good humour.

Later that day, when everyone else had gone, Khalid took his torch and walked out of the gatehouse, where the staff offices were located, to wander through the Elizabethan garden and up the stairs to the keep. Keep what? he wondered, shining a beam on the signboard that identified the building – but that didn't clarify the matter. Keep in? Keep out?

Some days it still struck him as miraculous that the English language, once a series of unbeautiful left to right squiggles on a page, was now a friend, opening one door after another for him in this country far from home. But in moments such as this – encountering a word that should mean something but obviously meant something else, and feeling inadequate for not being able to work it out – he remembered that the language would never be to him what it was to his sister. For her it was a great love, rich in riddles and double-meanings and ambiguities. She had delighted in it almost as soon as they started to learn it at the school set up in the early days of war, back when 'liberation' seemed a possible consequence of 'occupation'. *War backwards is raw! A group of crows is a murder! Where does the president keep his armies? Up his sleevies!* Some days he thought the reason she'd really been so angry when he left home to come here was because she was jealous that he would live in English, as she could never do. Switching off his torch, he turned and faced the garden. The moon was full, illuminating the marble fountain and the statues of the muzzled bears that felt like something from his old life. But his old life was far behind. Nothing told him this like these ruins formed by time, not bombs.

He switched the torch back on. He was a security guard without a gun, his presence enough to scare away any intruders – young lovers, teenagers in search of a dare. Here, even the ghosts were benign. He laughed softly, rapped his knuckles against the stone wall of the keep. 'Any ghosts here?' he called out, his voice echoing. No response, not even the wind through branches.

When midnight approached he was sitting on a low stone wall on the other side of the keep, finishing his careful reading of the guidebook. The moon had gone now and when he switched off his torch the structures all around him transformed from stone to concentrated darkness. A chill sliced through his bones.

Of course, the chill was brought on by the lateness of the hour, seeping even through his heavy jacket. He stood up, shook the pins and needles out of his hands and feet – he'd never sat in one place long enough to have pins and needles in both hands and both feet before – and approached the darkness, switching the torch back on just in time to see a single word rising up to meet his sight: 'FOREBODING'. He spun in a circle, the torchlight skittering over stone and grass and stone and when it came to rest on the signboard once more he saw that really it read 'FOREBUILDING', followed by a dense explanatory text.

'Idiot,' he said to himself, grinning. He wished he could call his sister to tell her about his mis-reading, but she hadn't spoken to him since he'd left – or, in her words, 'deserted' – their homeland. And there was no one else to whom he could comfortably reveal his fear who had enough English to appreciate the humour of the moment. He missed her, sharply, in that instant, but at least it was possible now to think of her without pain or guilt; she benefitted, along with the rest of his family, from the money he sent home, which would increase with this new job – his salary made magnificent by the currency exchange rates. His steps were confident, his tread light, as he set off, exploring.

Now that he knew their history, the ruins were transformed. He walked slowly through all the broken rooms where queens had danced and plots had been laid and kings had been insulted and marriage proposals that would have changed history were rejected and great feasts were prepared by those whose lives went unrecorded. How beautifully the star-filled sky took the place of stained-glass in the vast windows of the great hall.

Through the centuries, the men who owned this castle had in common their love of light. This was something he'd understood while reading through the guidebook. First a reference to the twelfth-century remarkably sized windows of the keep, then a mention of the fourteenth-century exceptionally high windows of the great hall, and following that a detailed description of the sixteenth-century light-flooding windows of Elizabeth I's private accommodation. Let in the light, and then let in more light.

A voice in Khalid's head – not his own voice, a woman's voice – said: *Did they love the light or was there something in the darkness they were trying to keep at bay?*

He shivered – it was the cold, nothing more, of course it was – and started back to the gatehouse, steps quickening.

✦

The alarm woke him up at eleven the next morning, in the attic room above the pub where he worked the afternoon shift. He sat up in bed, trying to ignore the protestations of his body to getting up so soon after lying down. The protestations of his mind were more insistent.

What kind of idiot is scared by ghost voices that he knows aren't there, and what kind of idiot sits outdoors reading on an October night in England. No wonder he'd woken up with a sore throat.

Despite gargling with salt water and sucking lemon-flavoured lozenges, the soreness hadn't receded by the evening and it was for that reason that he kept his perimeter walks to a minimum. He spent most of the night shift in the spacious staff kitchen of the gatehouse. He was at the kitchen table, reading one of the romance novels that were his guilty pleasure, when he smelled something he couldn't quite place, familiar but with a wrong note, like a flower just beginning to rot. He looked up at the window across from him, the one that rattled in its frame and was the likeliest way for a new scent to enter the room, but the smell was coming from behind him. It was both pleasant and unpleasant. He closed his eyes and put his hands over his ears to try and isolate it, and that's when he sensed it move. Not drift, not waft – move. The smell was coming towards him, attached to something – someone – that was now standing at his back. Khalid felt that old familiar weakness of his limbs – the one that said 'bomb' or 'someone breaking down the door' or 'why is my uncle lying down in his orchard away from the shade of a tree'. But this was England. He was in England, and the kitchen door must have opened without him hearing and someone had walked in, and was standing behind him, politely, waiting to be noticed. But the kitchen door creaked on its hinges; he would have heard it. And the presence behind him was so close. No one in England stood so close.

Turn around, he told himself, and a voice in his head – not his voice, a woman's voice – echoed, *Turn around.*

He would not turn around. Whatever happened, he must not turn around. He knew it the way you know a certain dog that you've always been on good terms with mustn't be approached – something about it was different. The word came to him again – *wrong.* He gripped the edges of his paperback. He would not turn around.

The only sound in the room was the ticking of the clock on the mantelpiece. It was going too slowly, two heartbeats of his between each second. *Tick dhu-dhug dhu-dhug Tick. Tick dhu-dhug dhu-dhug dhu-Tick.* He picked up his paperback and hurled it at the clock, knocked it onto the flagstones. Now there was only his heart and his breath disrupting the silence. The scent coming from behind him was so familiar – he tried to trace his way back through memory to find it – but the wrongness of it was a mask, irremovable.

'Whatever you are, whatever in this world you can possibly be, I've faced worse,' he said out loud. Saying it made him brave – no, more usefully, made him angry. He pressed the palms of his hands against the wooden table, felt the strength of an old oak tree enter him, and in one swift assured movement he stood up and turned around.

And the room turned with him. He was still facing the oak table and the rattling window. The scent still behind him. The thing, watching, still at his back.

He sat. Waited. This, also, he knew how to do. Wait through terror. Wait through your own impotence in the face of terror. Wait and hope it will be enough for terror to terrify you. On some days, the good days, that was all it needed.

✝

Much later – an hour? two hours? three? – he was still sitting tensed at the table, the thing so close he dared not lean back in his chair for fear of brushing against it. And then, abruptly, he was alone again. The presence simply lifted and vanished. He sniffed at the air. No trace remained of whatever had been there an instant ago. He inhaled deeply through his nose. Nothing had ever smelt sweeter than the stale coffee from his half-full mug and the dishwashing liquid from the uncapped bottle on the sink. His muscles untensed, his body allowing itself to feel its exhaustion. A short time later, Khalid fell asleep at the kitchen table.

When he woke he didn't know which memories of the previous night had been dreams and which had been brought on by the sickness he was incubating. His throat was sorer this morning – a bright star of pain behind his Adam's apple. He stood, swept up the broken pieces of the clock and waited for the property supervisor, who liked to arrive long before the rest of the staff, so he could apologise for the clock and ask where he might buy a replacement.

'No need for that,' she said, when he explained without explaining. 'It was a cheap old thing and anyway I have a spare one at home that'll just need a battery. Was it you that knocked it down or one of the ghosts?' She was smiling as she said it, but something in his expression made her come up to him and put a hand on his arm. 'It can be strange here at night,' she said. 'You know the gatehouse is where you'll find the most ghosts, not the castle.'

It was because the castle had so little left of its original doors and furnishing, she explained. Ghosts attached themselves to these things. Here in the gatehouse there were pieces brought from all over the property as well as original fittings. Leicester's fireplace, the Elizabethan staircase, bits of furniture. She walked him round, pointing out all the places where staff and visitors had met ghosts – the scent of tobacco so often in this room, the feeling of being watched on that landing, the stairs which creaked under the tread of something invisible. And that old wooden door – no one knew where it originally came from – behind which a group of visitors had once heard voices speaking in Spanish.

'Couldn't there have been Spanish speakers on the other side?'

'The door's always locked. I have the only key, but it hasn't been used since I started here fourteen years ago. I peeked inside just the once to see there was nothing in there worth seeing – just a storage room full of dust.'

He knew she was trying to reassure him and on another day perhaps he would have understood that it wasn't unusual to be carried away by your imagination in here – or encounter the inexplicable-but-harmless – but his throat ached terribly, exhaustion was deep in his bones, and the feeling of wrongness was still with him. What he wanted, needed, was familiarity. *Familialarity.* His sister had invented that term.

He excused himself from the company of the property supervisor and made his way upstairs to the oak-panelled room which was filled with early morning light, and allowed better mobile reception.

This wasn't the time he usually called home, and it was possible that everyone would be out – his father and cousins in their orchards, his mother and aunt cooking outdoors, his sister teaching at their old school. But his father answered on the second ring.

'Son?' his father said, in response to his respectful greeting. 'You're calling? You know already?'

'Know what?'

His sister was dead. A bomb had detonated in the school building. Perhaps attached to a human, perhaps not, did it matter? The windows had shattered and a piece of glass, like a spear, had cut right through her. They took her to the hospital but she had lost too much blood. This was yesterday – they were going to tell Khalid when he made his weekly call home tomorrow.

'Was she conscious in hospital?'

'Yes, at first.'

'You should have called me. We could have spoken.'

'The glass went through her neck, it severed the place that makes speaking possible.'

'Voice box,' Khalid said, in English, touching three fingers to his throat.

✦

A few minutes later he was back on the ground floor again, looking for the property supervisor to tell her he was sorry, she would have to find someone else for tonight, he had to go. Go where, he didn't know. Go to the airport, with the papers he now had that made returning here legal? Go to the city where he had cousins who could mourn with him? Go – away from here. That was all. Away from another night in this place with its silence so complete it made you hear voices in your head.

The property supervisor wasn't in the room with Leicester's fireplace where he'd left her; she wasn't in the staff kitchen. But as he went towards the stairs again, he saw the old wooden door was ajar. She must have decided to have another look in the storage room full of dust. He pushed the door open, and stepped inside. Something soft – cloying – caressed his head, the side of his face. He jumped back out into the hallway. Cobwebs, just cobwebs. He stepped in again, brushed them aside, called the property supervisor's name. No, she wasn't here. But how cold it was. He stepped forward, wanting to prove to himself that he wasn't afraid. It was an entirely unremarkable coldness in a stone-walled room without windows.

The door slammed shut behind him. No gap between door and doorframe to allow in even a sliver of daylight. That smell, previously out of memory's reach, bloomed in the darkness. He knew it now. It was ink and lemon and musky underarms; his sister's scent. And the mask pulled over it was blood, metallic and sharp.

The smell entered his nose and his mouth and the pores of his skin. It was almost a taste, almost a texture. His skin tightened on his bones, his tongue curled back on itself. *Turn around*, she dared him. But if he did that, the room would turn with him, the doorway forever at his back. He had never fallen for any of her tricks twice, not even when they were benign, before she blamed him for leaving, before he said *a man's job is to provide* and she replied *no, it's to protect; you're only leaving because it's safer and because you can.*

He glanced down at the phone in his hand. Of course, no signal. But on the other side of the door the property supervisor was calling his name. All he had to do was shout out a response, and she would find the key to the door, and let in the light and the living.

You can't keep me where I don't want to be whether you're alive or dead, he mentally addressed his sister. *I'm sorry.*

The property supervisor had come closer to the door. She called his name again. Pain lanced his throat as he yelled out to her. No sound emerged.

A voice in his head – not his voice, but one inflected just like it – said, *the doorway to this room, can you guess where it came from?* A giggle, then, all malignancy and triumph, *Well, I never could resist a word game, could I?*

The keep.

STUART
EVERS

NEVER
DEPARTED
MORE

In youth she imagined castles: far-away, fantastical, cold-stoned, improbably built castles. Turrets and battlements, mile-high keeps and bottomless moats, the standards of imaginary dynasties flagging in the wind, the sky always on the break of storm. In dark chambers her boot heels tapped the polished flags, her hands traced legends on wall-length tapestries, her swords slew ogres and giants and dragons. In grand halls she ate chicken legs and threw their bones to rascal dogs and pink-tailed rats; in cellars and oubliettes she rescued kings and queens, assisted by chain-mailed knights and white-smocked maidens. She felt the chill even at home in New Mexico's heat; the darkness even in its blind, persistent light.

In her early twenties now, a woman now, but one who had never seen a castle in any kind of proximity. The producer had given her the final say on the location. He wanted her to be comfortable. He wanted her to feel that the castle was *her* Elsinore. He had given her two choices: one in Serbia, the other in England. He provided photographs, spread them across the coffee table in his office. He pointed to the Serbian castle throughout; repeatedly said its name. She looked diligently at the photographs. It was in the English castle she saw herself; saw herself as a little girl, running the battlements, opening its doors, slaying the evil within. The producer asked if she was sure she was up to it. If she was really sure. He reminded her that this was her last chance. He reminded her that there was only so much he could do. He reminded her he was there to help, they were all there to help, should she ever need it.

A month before principal shooting on *Ophelia* was to begin, she asked for his help. She wanted to go on a week ahead. To get an understanding. To feel the aura. To immerse herself.

'In my madness will be method,' she said and waited for laughter that did not come. The producer didn't even smile: he looked genuinely alarmed.

'But you are doing so well here,' he said. 'Why not stay?'

'I will do just as well there. Don't you worry.'

He looked unconvinced, but she had been doing well, and so she deserved reward. He made some calls and booked her a cottage in the castle grounds. He insisted she take her assistant. To that she agreed. Her assistant was easily and often bought.

'We know what we are, but know not what we may be,' Maya said as she handed her assistant the cash and details of the London hotel. 'At the castle I will know what I may be. But not with you beside me. Thank you for understanding.'

The young woman nodded and got into her taxi. Maya watched it drive away. She felt already changed. In the back of the car she kept her eyes on the windows, looking for castles, those she had believed populated England just as drive-thrus and strip-malls had in New Mexico. She saw them too, just as she had imagined them, on hills looking down on the world below.

It was dusking when they arrived, the castle illuminated in greens and pinks, like it was lit for her, a personal beacon. At the gate, vast doors were pushed open by two uniformed men. The car followed a winding track, skirting the Great Tower, just inside the perimeter wall. Her driver said nothing, but she could not stop talking. 'Look at it,' she said, 'look on't!'

From the kitchen window of her cottage she could see the castle. She gazed at it for some time; the temerity of it, the very realness of it. She blew it a kiss. She investigated the welcome hamper and found a bottle of wine. She took it and a glass and let herself out of the cottage, crossed the pathway and leant on the perimeter wall, looked out over Dover. The sea was calm, boats in the distance. She glanced back to the castle, up at its vainglory and cuboid pomp. She saw the Union flag atop the battlements and imposed her own coat of arms on its unfurled stitching. She drank the wine and sang Ophelia's songs to the castle walls and her new-found Elsinore, sang until there was no more wine and the wind had chilled her enough to sleep.

The next day, in headscarf and dark glasses, she took tours of the Great Tower and tunnels, followed an injured World War II airman's progress through the underground hospital. She heard the legends and history and saw the shots, the scenes, the moments that would be filmed, that would capture her at an exact moment in time. She would be forever Ophelia, forever caught in that moment of inhabiting her, of bringing her vigorously to life. It was her. She was her. She felt herself slide into Ophelia, into the role, the familiar sensation of breaking down into something other.

Her assistant called after her nap, a quick, business-like exchange, confirming Maya's continued existence. Maya put down her phone and saw a van pull up outside the cottage, her grocery shopping for the week. She put on her dark glasses and let the driver unpack the wine and other items. He did not seem to know who she was.

'I'm having guests over tonight,' she said.

The man smiled and carried the empty crates back to the van.

She woke after ten. She ran the shower, but turned it off

without getting inside. Ophelia would not shower. Ophelia would smell of herself, not coconut and shea butter. She walked from the bathroom back to the master bedroom. From the wardrobe she took her costume. She had helped design it: a white shift, brocaded at the neck, brilliant blue and red flowers curling around her sternum, lace at the hem. She took the daisies she'd picked earlier in the day and arranged them in a crown on her twisted topknot.

'We know what we are, but know not what we may be,' she said, looking at herself in the mirror. She took a bottle from the fridge and let herself out the back door.

For over an hour, she circled the Great Tower, avoiding the more modern outposts of cafés and ice-cream parlours at the edge of the grounds. She ran through her lines. They'd lodged, these lines and scenes, in a way lines had not for many years. She needed no prompt, her voice was loud in the air; her theatre voice, an already effortless English accent, reached from deep in her abdomen. Spit flecked the cool air, her arms and hands animated and wild, even while holding the bottle. She stood at the entrance to the castle, under the coats of arms, looking up at the Great Tower, and in a tempest of words found Ophelia.

'He took me by the wrist and held me hard,' she shouted.

Again: 'He took me by the wrist and held me hard.' This time better. More spite, less bewilderment.

Again: 'He took me by the wrist.'

In the words she found an ire, a fury that broiled. She danced around in the night, frenzied in performance, and at the last, threw the empty wine bottle at the ground. It smashed loudly, shatteringly, and with delight she spat on its shards.

'I did repel his letters and denied his access to me,' she shouted, and left Maya behind for good, left her drunk and alone in the empty cottage.

She was on her knees, close, so close to the glass. She panted, exhausted by her efforts, and saw boots coming towards her, boots but no sound upon the gravel. She heard a voice, American, a shimmer to his words. Southern perhaps, a touch of the confederate about it.

'Is everything all right, ma'am?'

He stood there, concerned, rocking on shined boots. An airman's uniform, slick oiled hair, a face like a matinee idol, the kind of face men no longer possessed. She pushed herself up, dusted off her hands.

Were she Maya, she would have raged. She would have threatened. 'I was told there was no one here,' she would have said. 'They signed a piece of paper. They signed an NDA. Heads will roll for this. I tell you heads will roll!'

She would have said that, but the words, the very idea of the words, did not come. He walked towards her. She instinctively retreated, but didn't appear to move any further from him.

'Nothing to be frightened of, ma'am. I'm US Airforce. We're here to protect.'

'I'm not frightened, sir,' she said. 'There's nothing in you that could cause me fear. Surprise, perhaps, yes, but nothing else. You lack the height.'

He laughed, something almost see-through about the sound, as though, like a duck's quack, it would not echo.

She looked down at her dress. It was dirty, her knees were pitted with gravel, her fingers filthy. She straightened her back, brought her hands to her hips.

'Does the gentleman not introduce himself?'

'My apologies, ma'am. They call me Edward.'

She put her head to one side, an askance look.

'They call you Edward? Is that not your name, sir?'

'That's what they call me,' he said. 'And you, ma'am? How am I to address you?'

'You can call me Ophelia.'

His eyes narrowed; he put his head on one side.

'And is that not *your* name, ma'am?'

He took a few paces closer. He smelled of sandalwood and brier. He held out his hand. She looked at it. She took it and he kissed it. The touch was light but present, evident on her skin, a slight warmth from his lips.

'You sound American. Are you American, Ophelia?'

'I am not,' she said. 'Or if so, I am not aware of it.'

He looked downcast for a moment, lonesome, then looked back at her.

'I thought I detected a trace, but perhaps I am mistaken. I miss the sound of American women.'

He offered the crook of his arm.

'The view from the castle is so beautiful on a clear night. You can see France, the lights on the mainland shining. Would you like to see the lights, Ophelia?'

'There is melancholy in lights glimpsed from a distance,' she said. 'A party to which one has not been invited.'

He laughed.

'Is that a yes?'

She paused, but soon slipped her hand into his arm. They walked towards the castle. They saw France, its pin lights and glow. She leant her head on his shoulder and listened to him talk of how he had wished for company, real company, as the night wicked away and the sun blanched the crest of the tor.

✦

She woke in darkness, the whole of the day gone, dressed still in her Ophelia shift. It had not been uncommon, and she did not censure herself too much for it. She made coffee and ate a slice of mango. Her phone was in a cupboard; full immersion, no distractions. She read the script from start to finish, the words familiar as song. She ate another slice of mango and took a bottle of wine from the fridge, went out to see if she could find Edward again.

He was sitting on the wall, long legs dangling. She did not fall for men. They fell for her. Ophelia, though, different. A different age. A different time. Ophelia felt safe with him; saw refuge and safety in his arms. She did not question it. There was nothing to question. He held out his hand.

'My lady,' he said in gentle mockery. 'Woulds't thou walk with me a time?'

He jumped down from the wall. She laughed as he stumbled.

'I would be honoured, sir.'

'Well, to the castle we shall walk, and the elders there we will meet.'

'There are others, sir?'

'None as dear as you, ma'am, but more than you can imagine.'

With her arm in his they walked the incline, round the back of the Great Tower, entering it through a small door. It was chill, like the castles of her youth, but loud and flickering with torchlight. There was music playing, the sound of laughter and scuffles of feet. He led her impatiently through the chambers to the source, the heat rising with every corridor they traversed. Before the Great Hall, five men were playing cards and drinking whiskey, smoking filterless cigarettes, dressed like Edward. The men ignored them as they passed.

The Great Hall was sweltering, smoke-filled, men-and-women choked, the whole chamber at feast. Children scampered under tables, women pleasured men, a fight broke out and then rescinded. Red and blue and gold gleamed in the guttering light, food piled on tables was eaten or discarded to the straw beneath. The costumes were inconsistent. An airman danced with a girl in a wimple; two of Wellington's men were embroiled in a drinking competition with a medieval friar; a king talked sagely with a fat man dressed in Bermuda shorts and a t-shirt which read: 'I know I'm old, but at least I saw all the good bands'. Edward took her to a table and called to a young lad who brought them goblets and a jug of wine.

'The finest wine you'll ever taste,' he said.

She sipped from the goblet and it was like drinking for the very first time. A shiver of taste, damson and plum, then a hint of liquorice, of cinnamon and spice, then tobacco and chocolate. Men blew kisses towards her, but she demurred. Edward laughed his unechoing laugh and pointed out those he knew, their stories gruesome and tragic. He poured more wine and leant in closer to her. He smelled different tonight. Something smoky to him, something like diesel.

'And so how did *you* get here?' he said.

'I followed you, sir,' she said.

He wagged a finger.

'A fine answer. Now. Let's dance!'

Some of the airmen were playing trumpets, the assembled crowd dancing to toneless jazz. Edward held her close and she fell into those arms in a way she would never before have considered. His shirt was dirtier than the previous night. There were smudges on his skin. They danced and drank until, exhausted, they sat back at their table. He put his hand on hers and looked into her eyes; swimming, his eyes, fluid. They kissed. And oh, the collapsing world. A kiss, like the wine, that felt like the very first of its kind. When they broke their embrace, it felt as though she had been plucked from the sea, just at the moment of drowning.

He poured them more wine and was about to say something, but became distracted. She looked to where his eyes had flitted. A woman in a long red dress was walking through the hall. Ophelia watched her pick up a goblet, drain it and make her way towards the back of the room. As she reached the staircase, she turned and fixed

Edward with a pale gaze. Then she disappeared into the darkness.

'Who, pray, is the lady?' she asked. 'Her face could make a tyrant weep.'

He looked down at his goblet, put his fist around the stem, shook his head.

'It is a sad story, hers,' he said. 'She loved a man of privilege and position, but she was not of a high birth. They met in secrecy, lived as man and wife as much as was possible. He was sent to war, a war from which he did not come back. To join him, she threw herself from the castle walls. And now she is cursed to walk the Great Tower every night, waiting for something to set her free. The cruelty is, she doesn't know what that thing might be. We can all leave' – he extended his arm to the whole room – 'whenever we like. But not her. Or so the story goes. She's yoked to the place. Trapped. Imagine that.'

He looked down at his wine and finished it. He put his hand back on hers. His face changed from sadness to levity.

'So, Ophelia,' he said, 'how do you like our little house of debauchery?'

She poured more wine.

'I like it well enough, sir. Well enough indeed.'

✦

She dreamt she was banging on the doors of the castle, demanding entry, shouting for admittance. She woke to the same sound. At the door to the cottage was her assistant in a state of some alarm.

'What's the emergency?' Maya asked, her assistant pushing past her, looking in each room. She stopped in the kitchen. Maya followed. There were ants on the mango. Bottles on the floor, coffee spilled on the table.

'I've tried for two days to get hold of you,' she said.

'I've been here,' Maya said. 'Preparing. Getting into character.'

Her assistant passed her a phone. On it was a video of her smashing a wine bottle, shouting into the wind, talking animatedly to herself, trying to force her way into the castle, collapsing in a heap by its door and then hauling herself back up.

'You're lucky,' her assistant said, 'they didn't post it anywhere.'

Maya watched herself in the night, her hair untamed and wild; her dress almost black in places.

'I told you,' she said. 'This is preparation. And you've ruined it. Ruined it. The whole thing.'

Maya swept the debris from the table to the floor. Her assistant shook her head.

'You need help, Maya.'

'I need no such thing. I need you to leave and I need to prepare.'

The assistant picked up her phone.

'I'm going to have to tell the producer. You know that. You know what that means, don't you?'

'You must do whatever is in your heart and in your conscience,' Maya said, 'but now, leave. Out! Out!'

The assistant left. Maya went back to her bed. She slept until darkness fell.

✦

Ophelia took a bottle of wine and opened the door.

'Oh my lord. Edward!' she said.

Edward was standing by the wall, his tunic on fire, his face blackened with soot and ash, his hair smoking. He put his hand to his face.

'You see flames?' he said.

She ran to him, shook the wine over the flames, but they remained ablaze. He shook his head. A single tear cleaned a trough down his cheek.

'I'd hoped it would not happen this time. That our love would dim your eyes,' he said. 'But no.'

He walked towards her, put his hand on her shoulder.

'Our world is cruel, Ophelia. The few that can see us,

see us as we would like to be seen. In our pomp and grandeur. As we ourselves see each other. But it never lasts for long. The veil always lifts, and you see us as we really are. As we were at the moment of death. It's why we do not seek communion with the living. The disappointment is all too livid.'

He wiped his hand across his cheek. Some skin shed, scattered to the ground.

'We don't have much time,' he said coming to her, 'so let's go. The boys have promised something special tonight. Some new number they've been working on. It will be brilliant or terrible. Either way, it will be something to behold!'

He laughed but it came only from one side of his mouth. It sounded pained.

He crooked his arm. She put her hand through the flames. They were warm, like a child's breath, but did not burn or catch. They walked and they talked as though nothing had changed.

In the antechamber before the Great Hall, his fellow airmen were missing limbs. All were charred black. She could see one of their jawbones beneath scorched skin. At their usual table, the boy who brought the goblets and the wine was missing most of his skull. Wellington's men were open-gutted, the girl with the wimple riddled with pox. They seemed not to notice; their din and dancing as loud and as spirited as before. The woman in red walked past their table again; battered and bruised, bones broken and misshapen under her skin. Ophelia watched her pass. Suddenly, the woman turned and hissed at Ophelia, her face as red as her dress, her teeth smashed like old rock.

Edward was now entirely in flames, his skin blistered and cracked. He leant his hand across the table and she took it; she took his hand and was not afraid. Not afraid at all. And then was.

Ophelia began to cry. Cry with heave and weight in the stomach. To have lost him. To have had this time, and now to lose it so utterly, so damnably. She could not look at his face. Could not look at those around her, their deathly forms, their pain and suffering. She cried and she felt his hand on hers.

'Ophelia,' he said. 'We have loved, have we not?'

'Oh yes, Edward,' she said. 'We have loved. Oh we have loved, sir. And I am broken. I will die without you. I know that in my heart. Without you I will die.'

'You do not fear death?' he said. 'Not at all?'

'I have been nearer to death than anyone,' she said. 'Death has been a silent companion my whole life. One cannot fear such a close and constant kin.'

He sipped his wine. He leant in to her.

'Let me tell you what I can see. I see three men dressed in robes eating chicken legs. A soldier kissing a serving wench. A child stroking a kitten. Tell me, what do you see?'

She looked around the Great Hall. She saw three corpses gnawing at bones. A man with a chest wound bleeding on a slit-wristed woman, a boy with an umbilical cord around his neck holding a rat. She smiled.

'Oh, Edward,' she said. 'I can see it.'

'See what?' he said.

'I see the possibility,' she said, suddenly light. 'I see what needs to be done.'

'Oh, Ophelia,' he said, his face creasing. 'Oh, my love, no. I forbid it. I absolutely forbid it.'

She smiled and drank the last of her drink. She kissed him passionately on the mouth, her eyes closed and in remembrance of that first kiss, and ran to the staircase; Edward following behind, limping on his broken legs, dragging himself slowly after her.

✦

Atop the battlements she could see to France. She decided to head in that direction.

'Let in the maid, that out a maid, never departed more,' she said.

Oh the lightness of that rush! Oh the joy of that descent! Oh the sweet swell of love in amongst the breeze!

✦

She woke in the dark. There was distant, melancholy light. She shifted and looked around. She was in a bedchamber, one she'd seen before in the Great Tower. Rough stone walls and tapestries, a fire dying in the grate. She heard movement outside and then Edward was there, as he had been before: spruce and neat, a matinee idol in his airman's uniform, his hair oiled and perfectly parted, skin smooth and white. He sat down on the bed. He shifted a strand of hair from her eyes.

'Thank you,' he said. 'Thank you for this gift. This wonder. This salvation.'

She tried to kiss him, to push herself up. He placed his hand on her chest.

'You must rest,' he said. 'Stay there awhile.'

He got up and walked back towards the door as a woman wearing a white dress came through it. The woman placed her arm around Edward's waist.

'Thank you,' she said, in the direction of the bed. 'The years I have waited. The years I have waited for this moment.'

Edward put his arm around the woman's shoulder. He smiled. From the bed, she pushed herself up to standing.

'Edward?' she said. 'Edward?'

'Shhh,' he said. 'It's late.'

'Yes, it's late,' the woman said. 'It's late and it's time to walk.'

Their hands in each other's hands, they smiled at her and thanked her one last time. And then they left. They left her alone and aching. Alone, aching and wearing a long red dress.

KATE
CLANCHY

THE
WALL

The family therapist recommended a break, I write on the school's stern Term-time Absence Form.

I don't write: *since the fire I can no longer face the family home and even my daughter is desperate to leave it.* I don't need to: the school already knows about the fire. The firemen came to the school the day the kitchen went up, looking for Alison and her key. And afterwards, there were many more officials at school because arson is a crime and social workers and teachers have to be made aware. Though I think that arson is a big word for a fire in a bin; even if school books were the tinder.

Before the books were burnt, the teachers marked them, so they also think they know Alison. They know the Alison of the past six months, the pierced, pink-haired girl called 'Ali'. They know her books: the large, illiterate scrawl and the satirically wrong answers and the fantastical diary entries in the margins apparently written by an extra on *Home and Away*, 'Can't stay single any longer . . . Angie lent me her push-up bra'. Ali, who scrawls the word

Life in Gothic letters in red then scribbles out in big circles. Ali, who writes 'Ha! Ha!' under the teacher's bad marks, and then sets fire to the book.

I do not write, on the Term-time Absence Form, *I feel the need to drive away from this version of my daughter*, because the school believes the pink-haired girl is the real Alison, not a version. The school doesn't know the girl she was before, just eighteen months ago, the girl with plaits and a checked summer dress and arms full of library books; the girl with top marks and perfect spelling and round, careful, much-commended handwriting. That Alison has never appeared in this school, or at least, did not appear for more than a few months at the very beginning. I think that Alison's nice little friends from before – Oh, Eleanor, Martha, Nicola, of the skipping rope and gold stars, how I miss you! – do not believe in that Alison either, any more, so violent have the new Ali's verbal assaults been upon them, so far from arson and push-up bras are they.

What I have written on the form is not even true. When I said we were going away, and going to the Wall because we had been there before as a family, the therapist did not affirm us. Instead, she leaked out careful phrases: *the acceptance of routine and a new reality*, and *looking forwards not backwards*, and *accepting life as it is with all its mess*. But we did not listen: this is the kind of talk to make Simon shudder, and even I, who wanted to go to therapy, am sick of it now. The therapist herself is very tidy, with shiny reading glasses and small, wine-coloured cashmere cardigans, and so is her beige sofa and her carefully neutral room, and I don't believe that her life contains anything as messy as Alison, who spends most of the sessions hunkered forward on her new boots, picking her pink fringe, picking her painful, pierced nose, sighing like a Border collie kept too long inside.

I tried to tell the therapist about taking Alison to the Rollright Stones when she was six, carsick and whingey, how Simon brought two coat hangers with him. He paced Alison across the scrubby ground between the small mossy stones. He was tall as a druid in his old anorak, she was tiny as a toadstool in her red coat, and sure enough the magic worked: the unfolded coat hangers twitched and crossed in her small fat hands each time she crossed the ley line. They walked across the stones a hundred times and she budded out of her dark mood like a snowdrop from the earth and believed she was a good witch for a year.

'But Alison is a different girl, now,' said the therapist. And she is, but that smaller snowdrop girl is somewhere inside her, I believe, and I am sure Simon believes too. I think our beliefs are important and with all that is going on, arson and social workers and therapy-speak, they have been too much overlooked. Simon and I may not believe in God, but we do believe in History. As Simon says, the past is not an escape, it is a world full of lessons; where else can we learn? Simon believes the past heals. He has a particular feeling for the past embodied in a landscape, like the Rollright Stones. He says: landscape has its own mysteries and cures. There are places whose mere names make him push up his glasses and run his fingers through his hair and it makes me happy, correspondingly happy, to see him do this. We say the names together: Malmesbury; Caerleon; Glastonbury Tor.

Simon says: 'Hadrian's Wall is better than China. It's as good as the pyramids.' And I agree. So we are going, and I write on the form: *This is an educational destination*, which is true, and, *I will supervise homework*, which is a lie, and I sign. Probably none of this is necessary, neither the lies nor the truths. Probably, the form will go through on the nod. Probably, the school will be pleased to be rid of Alison for a day or two, in the same way that Alison will accept even this trip to get away from school, and this thought, that someone does not want my daughter, cuts to the core of me.

So we go to the Wall. We drive, and it is a long way and a lonely way, with Simon silent for all of it and Alison plugged into her headphones and peering at her phone with her hood over her head, even when we stop to eat at the service stations. And I have forgotten how, when it rains in the North East, it rains like television, a broken one, the windscreen nothing but dark with flashes. There is no stopping on the way at the Temple of Mithras, as I'd hoped. We get to the hostel at Once Brewed in the dark, run for the door with our coats over our heads.

I've forgotten about hostels too, about the women's dormitory where Alison and I must sleep, sharing the room with two hearty German girls who were going to walk St Oswald's Way. Alison is still young enough to sleep anywhere, but I lie awake all night under the bulge of her body in the bunk above and think how unfair it is to be so lonely. I am so angry to be stuck in the women's dorm when I so very much dislike womanish things – periods, piercings, push-up bras – myself. I do not see why it should be me, and not Simon, who has to help her with all this now.

The next day it's not raining but there is a cloud sitting on the long valley where, according to my memory and the map, we are. Outside the hostel is a perfect whiteout: we can scarcely see the road, and the pub next door looms at us unexpectedly like an untethered mystical castle. It is early, though, only eight o'clock, and in the lost time of our family Simon would have said, 'It'll soon clear up, Ali. Tell me when you can see enough blue to make a pair of sailor's trousers,' and Alison would have smiled. Then we would have sat and played Go Fish at the varnished pine table, the three of us, with extra cups of coffee and hot chocolate for Alison, waiting till the cloud lifted, or Simon would have played chess with his daughter, with the little portable chess set we kept for such outings, the one with pieces so small he had to put his reading glasses on to distinguish knight from pawn, but Alison doesn't play games any more, and doesn't smile and doesn't believe in sailor's trousers, and within five minutes of breakfast I find I am unable to sit with her and the tinny scratching of her earphones and I bundle us into the car.

I drive very slowly at first with all my lights on. But the fog starts to lift almost at once, the worn gold hills revealing themselves on either side. 'Of course, it is a Roman road,' Simon says, in my ear. 'You can tell, it is so very straight.' I smile to hear him, and by the time we get to the turn-off to Housesteads, the weather is fine, really fine, a marvellous day for so early in the spring, the sky blowing itself high and clear, the long valley clearing east and west. We can see the fort written in grey on the ridge of the hill above the car park, the mist just lifting from it.

I remember the Wall from here, because we all three walked it during our very best summer, the summer Alison was nine. Just along from the fort is a milecastle with an arched entrance missing only its capstone, and most of the way the Wall is higher than your shoulder, and neatly faced with square cut stones. Suddenly, I'm desperate to be up there in the sun and wind, desperate to be with Simon, out walking. I can see us, both of us in our light expensive walking boots and neoprene jackets, him outlining the place where buildings sleep under a blanket of turf with his long brown hands and the walking pole we bought in Austria.

But Alison won't come. Alison has changed her mind about the holiday, and the Wall, and seeing anything, and will not put on her walking boots. She won't even move from the back seat where she is doubled up over her phone to shut out the light. 'I'm watching a video,' she shouts, 'a video.' And when I pull her she knots herself tight as an embryo, a conch, and is too heavy to lift. When you are with a teenager you become a teenager, just as when you are with a two year old you have tantrums. I hear myself yell: 'I'll go on my own, my own.' And I do, I run up the track in my boots, gasping at the turns, flighting the birds.

And so I am here alone in the fort. There is a fine high sound of larks, and a thin cool wind, and no one here at all: too early in the day and the season for even the museum to be open, to even buy a ticket. I like the museum. There are models of the fort in its different incarnations, and a few small artefacts including a carving of three hooded figures wearing what look like anoraks, and a sign explaining that the coats are good quality woven wool, a very British product.

I decide not to care about Alison for a while. I will calm down and take myself on a tour. I don't have my guidebook, but I remember. I walk up through the outlines of the town outside the boundary wall of the fort, remembering. In one of these houses they found the bones of a woman and a man, the man with a dagger between his ribs, both hidden beneath the clay of the floor like the body under the patio in *Brookside*.

I go into the fort through the south gate, past the worn cart tracks and postern hole, and clamber on past the outline of the commanding officer's house to the hospital. This is my favourite spot. It is so easy to imagine the clean, small, tiled courtyard with its deep-set drainage, its cold larder of medicines and its neat, offset latrine. I can feel what it would have been like to have been brought in here, broken or damaged from fighting, into a cool, lime-washed cell, and lie under a woollen blanket until you healed, or not. The Romans knew about bone setting, and cauterising and stitching wounds: so many things we forgot afterwards.

I sit on a stone. And the view from here is magnificent: the Wall thrusting itself east up the backbone of the hill, purposeful and unflinching as a great scaled snake. In the other direction, down in the valley, I see that Simon has finally taken action, and is walking Alison up the track from the car park. He has even induced her to put her coat on and push her hood back, though not, I see, to put her boots on. He'll take her round to the east gate, I know, insist that she enter the fort from the 'proper' side, through the double-arched gateway the Romans planned; the gate that leads you in to face the headquarters with its pillars and offices and gods; the gate built to impress the people and be exactly Roman. Later, they blocked up one of its arches and built a coal store in the passageway; people started to use the south gate more because it was easier, and out of the wind, nearer the *vicus*, the town, the way people always untidily will.

I like the town, myself: its irregular, un-Roman buildings built into the folds of the hill; its murder victims; its loaded dice and counterfeit coins; all the untidy compromises of it. I like all the evidence of the later, unplanned, inner fort too; everything that happened as the empire decayed: the grim barrack dormitories made over into wooden huts to hold a family each, the chilly open porticos in headquarters closed off against the sea winds and turned into warm little offices for probably corrupt officials. It's like a family wearing in a home, or a religion settling on some comfortable hypocrisies; or a marriage finding its own perverse, beloved shape.

The bathhouse was built late on, I remember, inside the fort because it was getting too dangerous to go outside for a bath. It is also very small. It takes me five minutes to even find it: it can't have fitted more than two or three people at a time. But it is so complete that you can still see the stains on the underfloor heating and the place where the boiler fitted. The scorch marks bring them very near: the anxious Romans desperate to remember what warmth felt like; the servant trained to stoke the boiler; the cart loaded with coal bouncing along the military road all the way from Newcastle; the man who drove the cart, whose precious business it was.

Now Alison has come inside the bounds of the fort. She is only a hundred yards from me now, in the latrines in the far corner, but I don't call out or try to join her: I want to watch her. She's actually smiling. It's because her father is there, smiling too, the wind feathering his soft brown hair, the sun wrinkling his soft brown skin, leaning back on the stones, explaining it all to his Ali. How it all works. The cistern of rainwater above the latrine, with its smooth-worn washing stone and still-functional channel, there to power the flush. The latrine itself, with its wash basins and water channel to wash out your sponge, its deep, solid, sloping drain.

The loss of it all, when you think about it, is inconceivable. How can it be that the latrine was allowed to fill up with gravel and mud, and that people simply forgot how to beat copper and set bones and dry corn and make hypocausts? How can it be that in the year 400 there was a coal-fired sauna here, with a copper boiler, and a granary with under-floor heating, and the infrastructure to serve all of it, and then it was all smashed and fell down and nothing was built for a thousand years till some starving Scots made a messy fort from the stone of the south gate, a primitive tower without chimney or internal stair? It must be as Simon always says, the weather must have changed, the climate. Something fundamental must have happened. A death.

Anyway. I walk down to Alison. She is sitting on a wall, softly kicking her trainers on it, holding up her face to the bit of sun. Her eyes are shut, but when I come over she opens them.

'Mum,' she says, 'Dad was here.'

'I know,' I say. 'I saw him.'

'I miss him,' said Alison. 'I miss my dad. Do you miss him? What do you feel? I don't know what you feel.'

What do I feel? In all the months since Simon's death, she has not once asked me that.

I tell her I feel like a body stabbed and buried under the clay of a ruined house, or like a postern hole worn in a stone, empty, or like a young soldier shivering in the lime-washed cell of the hospital, or like a wool cloak with a stiff hood, hung up on a peg, empty, empty.

'Sorry, Ali,' I say. 'I'm really sorry he died.'

'I didn't set fire to the bin on purpose,' she says. 'I was actually trying to put the fire out.'

But I knew that already. It is still early, so after a while my daughter and I walk out on the west side of the fort and start following the Wall to Steel Rigg. On the way we can see the milecastle with its nearly perfect arch, and the sycamore that grows in Sycamore Gap, and the beautiful wild country stretching out to Kielder that in Roman times teemed with game. The wild Picts are gone now, and the wolves, and the beaver and the otter, and the deer flying through the woods from the huntsman like seeds blown from a palm, and now Simon, my husband, Ali's father, is gone too; but the cliffs, and the high sky and white clouds, and the land and the water and the Wall thrusting through it; all of that is still there.

JEANETTE WINTERSON

AS STRONG AS DEATH

The town of Falmouth . . . is no great ways from the sea. It is defended on the sea-side by tway castles, St Maws and Pendennis, extremely well calculated for annoying every body except an enemy . . . The town contains many Quakers and salt fish – the oysters have a taste of copper, owing to the soil of a mining country – the women . . . are flogged at the cart's tail when they pick and steal, as happened to one of the fair sex yesterday noon. She was pertinacious in her behaviour, and damned the mayor. (Lord Byron, Falmouth, 1809)

I put down the book to visit the bathroom.

I was alone that night. For the three nights of our wedding party, Tamara and I had decided to follow the custom of sleeping separately until the night of the wedding. It was her idea – to create a space where we longed to be, and then to find it.

I'd been drinking with our friends. I'd gone to bed late. I couldn't sleep, so I was sitting propped up on my pillows, reading about the history of the place.

As I opened the heavy square-panelled door to the bathroom, I heard a voice say, 'Go through and don't come back.'

I turned on the bathroom light. Stood still. No sound.

It was an old-fashioned bathroom with a tall sash window pushed up a little at the bottom. I pushed it up further, feeling its weight, and leaned out into the night. The night was blustery and restless. The wind like a conversation you can't hear. No stars. A little way off, towards the castle itself, I saw a wavering light, dim and unsteady.

I smiled – it must have been a couple of our guests zig-zagging home from drinking. I must have heard them through the window. It's so quiet here. That's why the voice seemed so close, even though the light seems far away.

But the sea and the night make things mysterious, don't they?

My wife was born in Falmouth. That is why we chose to marry at Pendennis Castle. The castle and its pair at St Mawes face each other across the mouth of the River Fal, like stone giants guarding a hoard.

Henry VIII built a blockhouse either side of the estuary to cross-fire any enemy ships slinking through the water. Henry worried about the war-ish Spanish and his daughter Elizabeth saw off the Armada, but it was Bonaparte, with his eyes on the prize of a coastal landing, who galvanised the British into building up their bullish garrison here, the booming guns aiming their cannonballs at history. The sea-floor of the bay is thick-deep with them. Pendennis was defended by twenty-two 24-pounders and fourteen 18-pounders.

'It's a castle not a burger-chain.'

'Tamara, that's what they call them – pounders.'

'I like to think of all those tin soldiers eating mayo and fries with their 24-pounders.'

'Are you making fun of history or making fun of me?'

'You. That's why we're getting married – so that I can laugh at you for the rest of my life.'

Morning. Drinking tea in her room. She's sitting up in bed and I am in a chair by the window.

'There's nothing you can tell me about Pendennis Castle that I don't know. My dad was a tour guide here for years.'

'I'm sorry he can't be here today.'

'He'll be here in spirit.'

'Maybe he will. It's Hallowe'en.'

'You don't believe in ghosts, do you?'

*

She came and sat on my knee, kissing me. Her eyes are grey, like the sky over the sea today, and behind them, not always visible, but always there, is the sun.

'Someone came into my room last night.'

'It wasn't me.'

She said – 'The rain was heavy and it woke me – or I think it was the rain. I knew that someone was sitting on the edge of the bed looking at me.'

'How did you know that?'

'We all know when we're being looked at.'

'You were dreaming.'

'I wasn't dreaming. It was Dad.'

'How do you know?'

'Who else would it be?'

I'm thinking, This is ridiculous. She doesn't really believe in ghosts and neither do I. Yet what harm can it do if she believes her father came last night to wish her well? And the fact is that none of us has the slightest knowledge of what happens after we die.

Materialists are no better informed than mediums.

'Shall we go for a walk? While everyone else is asleep?'

She goes to wash and dress. I know her routine, her sounds, her movements, so well. But today I'm listening like she's new to me. I don't want to get used to her. I don't want to lose her to habit.

She comes out of the bathroom, hair tied back, smiling. She takes my hand. She's warm.

We walked under the gun-metal sky towards the oldest part of the estate. The Tudor fort is so small. Like a toy fort for toy soldiers. Time set in stone. So much time has happened here – not only months and years, not only time passing, but time happening.

Prince Charles hid here in 1646 during the English Civil War, on his way to safety in the Scilly Isles. He had his own door put into the castle. It's blocked up now, but the outline is there. Is the door blocked up when we're dead? Our own personal space–time door, that opens when we're born, and opens for us once more when we die?

Go through. Don't come back.

'What did you say?'

'I was thinking about the door.'

'Go through. Don't come back . . . that's what you said.'

'Did I? Oh. Someone was wandering round outside my room last night – something about a door.'

Tamara looked at me strangely. 'I'm cold.'

'Me too. It's this wind. Let's go into the castle.'

*

We walked through the rooms still panelled out the Georgian way, where an officer in white breeches and a cut-away coat could stand with his back towards the wood-burning fireplace and study a map of the French positions.

When Nelson was killed at the Battle of Trafalgar, the news was sent by ship to Falmouth, and a rider horsed up in a gale and set off for London to tell the King.

Life and death. You feel it here. I'm not superstitious but you feel it here.

On the wall of the modest sitting room there's a portrait of Captain Philip Melvill, governor of Pendennis Castle from 1797 until his death in 1811.

Something happened to him in India, they say, when he was imprisoned for four years in Bangalore. He suffered from extremes of emotion, so they say, a man as volatile as the weather here; a man of scudding clouds and flashes of lightning. The fog so thick on him sometimes he didn't know his own face.

He sat in the window in a comb-back Windsor chair watching the weather and the water. The tour guides have all heard him scraping the chair across the floor.

And some say that if you move the chair away from the window at night, by morning it will have returned to its place.

*

You've gone ahead, out of the castle into the wind, your slight frame struggling to stay upright. I'm following you. We won't live forever. We'll both disappear back into time, through our separate doors, and if you go first I won't be able to find you. I'll run my hands over and over the wall where the door used to be; you coming home, you coming in, the door you opened for me, so unexpected and welcome. The door into the sun.

Now is all we have. Stay in sight of me.

TAMARA!
  JAMIE!

She's gone through the tunnel towards Half-Moon Battery. We scared ourselves silly last night with our friends, imagining we heard the sound of boots marching past in step. In a place like this, layered like a fossil record through seams of time, it's easy to believe that time is simultaneous.

If haunting is anything, perhaps that's what it is; time in the wrong place.

The clock was striking. You turned to me, your face soft and serious. You said, 'I want to marry you, Jamie.'

'You are marrying me.'

'I woke up feeling – I don't know – uneasy.'

'It's just nerves. I hardly slept.'

'Really?'

She put her arms round me and rested her head on my shoulder.

And then I felt it distinctly; a lowering weight, a sinking motion, something pressing behind me in between my shoulder blades, exactly as if someone were leaning their forehead against me.

Tamara said, 'I like it when you put your hands on my hipbones.'

My hands were by my sides. I didn't tell her that, or that the space between my shoulder blades was cold and wet.

'Shall we go?'

My arm round her now, we set off walking back to our quarters. Soon it would be the beginning of our life together. We had been together a while but this felt different. We're both nervous, I thought. We're both imagining things.

As we went past the Battery Observation Post, closed to visitors today, and deserted in the early morning rain, the phone started ringing. I jumped sideways. Tamara laughed, opened the door, and pulled me inside, kissing me, suddenly, passionately, under the low roof, against the long horizontal windscreen window, while the Bakelite phone shrilled on the desk. 'It's part of the tour,' she said, 'a sound installation.'

The room had been re-made to look as it would have done during the Second World War; tin hats and mugs, flashlights, kitbags, charts, radio equipment. Crackling voices barked orders through hidden speakers.

The Morse code machine beeped into life. 'That's new,' you said.

DOT DASH DOT DASH DASH . . .

The staccato, urgent, high-pitched monotone coming from the metal box was producing a ticker-tape roll with the dots and dashes written on it. We both watched it, mesmerised and unsure. The beeping stopped as suddenly as it had started. Impulsively I tore off the roll. 'Can you read it?'

'No, but Uncle Alec will be at the party. He was in the Navy and he's about a hundred years old. Show it to him, he'll love it. Probably says "Welcome to Pendennis Castle".'

We ran back through the wind and rain towards breakfast and friends and laughter and the pleasure of the unfolding day. I went upstairs to dump my wet jacket, and decided on a warmer sweater. As I pulled off what I had on, I felt the cold dampness of where the head had rested on me. But it wasn't a head, was it? A head needs a body, and there was no-body-there.

A sudden gust of wind slammed the bathroom door.

*

'Oh, the Killigrews – yes, they were all pirates. The women as well as the men. Roaring girls, the lot of them. Line died out in the seventeenth century. No men left. Not that that would be a problem for you, my dear, eh? Ha ha ha.'

Tamara's Uncle Alec. That's what happens at weddings. He's trying to be friendly, I tell myself. It's not easy that his niece is marrying a woman.

'Kitty Killigrew dressed herself as a boy and went to sea, she did. That was just about all right, she was tall enough and flat enough to get away with it – figure more like an ironing board than an hourglass, if you get my meaning, but then, damn it if she didn't come home and start carrying on with a girl from the village, one of the oyster pickers. Well, that wouldn't do for a start and it certainly wouldn't do for a finish. Times were different then, y'know.'

'What happened to her?'

'Oh, terrible, terrible. Make your blood run cold. Not the thing for a wedding party. Not at all . . .'

'Why are you telling it to me then?'

The uncle looked surprised, like a man who has got on the wrong train. 'Am I? Well, perhaps I am. No truth in it at all, besides. A silly story.'

'Can you read Morse code?' I said, trying to change the subject. But Uncle Alec was deaf.

'Couldn't be happier for you, y'know, I had a friend just the same, oh, years ago; it's always gone on, of course, 'course it has, men and men, women and women, but marriage is a bit of a surprise, don't y'think? I mean, where does it end? If you don't draw a line somewhere? I daresay I'll be able to marry my dog.'

'Poor dog,' I said.

'Y'what?'

I got up. I didn't want to pick a fight with one of my new relatives.

The rest of the day passed happily. More friends were arriving. Tonight we were having the party, and the next morning, on All Hallows' Eve, we were to be married.

We had agreed that we would spend some quiet time together before the party. The celebrant wanted to speak to us about our commitment, and it felt right to take a couple of hours to think about our marriage together. I'd been out for lunch with my best woman and I was late.

As I was running towards the hall, I saw Tamara, up ahead of me, walking with someone; a tall young man in boots, buff trousers and a red coat.

They had rounded the corner before I caught up with them.

'TAMARA!'

She turned. She was alone.

'Who was that?'

She looked puzzled. 'Who?'

'You were with someone.'

'No, I wasn't. I was with Sara earlier but . . .'

'A man . . .'

'Jamie – this was meant to be a serious time – first, you're late, and second, don't play jokes on me. I'm going upstairs.'

'Tamara!'

I followed her. She went into her room without looking at me. I decided to give her a minute to cool off. My own room was just down the corridor.

Might as well unpack my wedding outfit.

I opened my wedding bag, everything pressed and folded, and separate to my other clothes. Neatly on the top of the plastic cover lay a chipped brass button – a uniform button. I picked it up and took it to the window. There was an inscription written round the edge: 'PUER SEMPER SEMPER PUELLA'.

I went straight back to Tamara's room. She was standing at the window looking out.

'There's the boy in the red coat,' she said.

'I can't see anyone.'

'He must have gone into the keep. I have no idea who he is.'

She was ignoring me, staring intently out into the grounds as though the empty space could yield something. I put the button in her hand.

'What does this mean?' She turned it between her fingers, frowning. 'Where did you get it?'

'It was in my luggage!'

'It means "Forever a Boy Always a Girl".'

'What does that mean?'

She laughed. 'Someone's playing a joke on us. Well, you are a girl who's a boy who's a boy who's a girl, or whatever happens in all those Shakespeare plays.'

She kissed me on my nose. 'It's probably Uncle Alec. He's doing his best but he's struggling.'

We were close again. She was in my arms.

The party was a success. Tamara had booked a seven-piece band called The Deloreans. Something about going back to our future.

'I feel like I've always known you,' she said.

'You never told me you believed in reincarnation as well as ghosts.'

'I don't,' she said. 'But I know you.'

Uncle Alec was drunk when I bumped into him later. He pulled me down into a chair. 'They shot her, y'know, bad business.'

'Shot who?'

'Kitty. The girl who's a boy . . .'

'Who's a boy who's a girl . . .'

'Count yourself lucky.'

'I do . . . for marrying Tamara.'

'The other one drowned herself. Dredged off the bottom of the sea. Told you it wasn't a wedding story.'

Whether the story put a dampener on my spirits or whether I was just tired, I kissed Tamara goodnight and went to bed. I fell asleep at once; a deep and dreamless sleep.

I awoke somewhere in the dead of night. The back of my neck was clammy. I must have been sweating but the room felt so cold. I half sat up on my elbows. The air in the room was heavy with moisture. I wiped a hand over my head – why was my hair clinging to my scalp? And what was that smell? The smell of seaweed . . .

I turned sideways into the middle of the bed and that's when I felt it: an arm. A body. A wet arm. A wet body. In spite of myself I ran my hand over the still form that lay beside me. The body I felt was soaked with water, pulpy, like something that has lain too long in water. And then I felt its face and the hollow sockets of its eyes.

I didn't scream. I couldn't. Whimpering, like something

whipped, I managed to get out of bed and over to the window. I opened the curtains. The moon was bright. Looking back towards the bed, I saw it was empty. Empty.

But as I looked out of the window I saw Tamara, like a sleep-walker, making her way towards the castle.

'TAMARA!'

By the time I caught up with her she was inside the castle gateway. The castle was dimly lit. There were flares on the walls.

Tamara looked at me, as if waking.

'Where are we?'

Before I could answer her the tall young man in the red coat came behind us. He was carrying a cocked hat and wearing a pistol at his belt. He seemed not to see us. I went towards him, and he brushed his hand in front of his face, as though he felt my movement but not myself.

There was a sound from behind and a young woman, hidden entirely in a cloak, ran into the room and threw off her hood. Even in the dim light of the flares I could see how beautiful she was, but her face was afraid.

She threw her arms round the young man. He took out a ring and put it on her finger. Then together they kneeled down, facing each other, and began to recite their wedding vows . . . with this ring I thee wed, with my body I thee worship . . .

'Death will not part us,' she said. 'Love is . . .'

She did not finish what she had to say. A posse of men stormed the room. The boy – he was hardly more than a boy – reached for his pistol but he was speedily overpowered.

'Run!' he shouted.

She ran – they seemed not to care – it was him they wanted. Hands behind his back, they shoved him forwards, up the stairs. I followed. I knew they could not see me.

Upstairs, the door. The door that opens into time. They pushed him out, through, I heard a shot and smelled powder, acrid and raw. And these words:

'Go through, and don't come back.'

And then it was done. The castle was dark.

Holding each other tightly, we stepped out of the castle. A voice said – 'Saw them, damn it, did you?'

It was Uncle Alec.

We were drinking whisky all three of us, long into that night. The spirits of murdered Kitty and her girl were known to walk abroad and to act again the terrible night of their parting.

'I can see them all, y'know, ghosts,' said Uncle Alec. 'Have done since I was a boy.'

'What should we do?' said Tamara.

Uncle Alec thought a while, and then he said, 'Invite them to the wedding.'

'How do we do that?' I said. 'They're dead.'

'Death never stopped anyone,' said Uncle Alec.

The morning of our wedding.

I had not slept at all, but lain wide-awake with Tamara sleeping in my arms. Is there a door between life and death? Are life and death as separated as we believe?

The morning of the wedding.

I bathed and dressed. On my table lay the button and the ticker tape of Morse code. I picked up the button, rubbed it between my fingers. 'Come with us,' I said. 'Into a time that is not death.' Then I left the button on the table, put the paper in my pocket, and went downstairs, where our guests were waiting in the hall.

The morning of our wedding.

I stood next to Tamara, holding her hand while we made our vows. As we turned to face each other, we each looked over the other's shoulder, and we both saw, one behind her, one behind me, the young man in the red coat and the beautiful woman whose hair spread out like the sea.

It was afterwards, though, that I gave the ticker tape of Morse code to Uncle Alec. 'Where'd y'get this?' he said.

'What does it say?'

'Love is as strong as death.'

MAX
PORTER

MRS CHARBURY
AT ELTHAM

'Who is the man in a brown cloak standing at the foot of my bed every night?' my sister asked, aged six or seven.

I said 'A ghost' and Mother said 'Bad dreams' and Papa said 'Absolute nonsense. Nobody cares for your made-up terrors.'

Papa died and we were a house of women. We grew accustomed, but not sympathetic, to Delia's unnerving claims.

She sometimes said 'That's him!' in a gallery, or in a busy street, and she would be referring to her man in brown robes. Once we rushed upstairs upon hearing her scream and she was pointing to the chair beside her bed.
'He was sitting in my chair!'

✦

I am standing on the gravel driveway of Eltham Palace. Someone called Rory Kippax from English Heritage has agreed to show me around, but he is late. My taxi has gone and it's drizzling. I am very elderly and I do not like rain, or waiting. I cannot tolerate lateness.

I shall give them until midday. Perhaps I shall cancel my membership.

Delia was fussing.

'Something is wrong with Eltham Palace' she said *'nothing good will come of me going there. I'd like to stay home and work on my paintings.'*

'Oh, fortify yourself Delia. Mummy is ill, and we have been invited, and the Courtaulds expect us, so we are going. You can't idle your life away, scuffing away at your naïve little pictures.'

Almost noon and still nobody here. I notice the huge wooden doors are ajar.

I bang on the door with my walking stick. I poke my head through.

'Hello?'

I wander in. It's freezing cold.

'Hello? Mrs Charbury here, I have a visit booked!'

I peer into the lavatories.

Oh yes, I remember these ghastly silver taps. *Moderne* design, sharp and angled, no doubt hugely fashionable back then, but one couldn't fit one's hand under to get any water. Typical of those people.

I did love the heated towel rails though.

'I don't like it' said Delia.

'Oh do shut up.'

And there we were, drying our hands and prettying our-selves, when we heard Virginia say to someone or other *'Yes, and I've just seen the Bush Sisters arrive. Ye-e-e-es, exactly. One beautiful and silly, one strange and ugly. One Flaming June berry, one burnt brûlée berry.'*

And I know Delia heard, because she blushed and hastened her efforts with the handwashing. Poor peculiar Delia. Dumpy and glum.

I step through into the domed room with its fly's eye roof; the pride and joy of New Eltham.

'Hello? Is anybody here?'

Back then I called it the Temple of Questionable Taste. I was jealous, I suppose.

'Hello?' I call. The building hums.

I think I can hear footsteps approaching so I peer expec-tantly down each corridor but nobody comes.

'Hello?'

There was champagne, so much champagne. Chatter and shrieks of laughter. Cigar smoke. Jazz. Silk.

'I don't like it here' Delia said to me. *'I have a very bad feeling.'*
I flounced off to flirt and dance and get sloshed.

I was terribly drunk all the time back then. We all were. I smoked until I couldn't swallow. At Eltham they topped you up all the time. There was nowhere you could go where people wouldn't pop up from behind some door, a grinning servant with more drinks, more options for intoxication.

'Dubonnet Cassis Madame?'
'Too bloody right, yes please.'

I was young and comely and we were invited to parties where very famous people gathered and got drunk. I loved getting sozzled with the well-to-do.

'Welcome to HMS Vulgar Italiano' someone said.

'Haha!'

There is no champagne today. Just the huge circular rug, browns and beiges and cruise-ship lines. I wonder why on earth Rory Kippax isn't here.

I wander down the corridor to the medieval great hall. It's deserted. I call out as I go through 'Hello?'

I said *'Virginia and Stephen!'* and she said *'Ginie, please!'* and my pitiful socialite spirit soared into the hammer beams above us.

I don't remember the hall being this big. I remember it being crammed with sticky bodies. Always so fiendishly hot. I remember people whispering *'Rab Butler is here!'*

Delia was next to me, stiff as a board. *'There is something wrong with Eltham. I don't feel well. There's something wrong.'* Someone said *'Quickstep!'* and I shrieked and whooped and ran away from Delia.

Someone said *'Edith Sitwell's dreadful poems'* and I said *'Oh spare me!'*

Someone said *'Taste does not come by chance: it is a long and laborious task to acquire it'* and all us slender dreadful ladies cackled.

They had a fetish for electricity and for warmth. A beautiful woman in green velvet slippers said to me *'The floor is warmer than a granite boulder in midsummer sun. Underfloor heating, no expense spared!'*

The floor today is ice cold. There are bits of old confetti stuck to the flagstones. This place is a party venue for hire. Was it ever thus.

I call out into the medieval emptiness 'Hello?'

I picture Delia crossing the huge floor to tell me she's scared, or worried. I imagine Edward IV spying on me from behind a curtain. Sinister history here. I feel a ripple of fear, all alone in this hall of memories, so I shout 'Hello!' and my sudden nervousness is embarrassing so I shut it off with noise, yelling 'HELLO!' yelling 'Is there anybody here? I have an appointment.'

I feel suddenly very self-aware. I wish I hadn't made noise. I feel perhaps I've woken the house up and that wasn't wise.

A man in a jester's costume said *'Refill, saucy Mixy?'*

I was rather too hot and dizzy and I was in something of a clinch I think, with a racing driver, a friend of the famous Italian nephews, and suddenly Delia was there, and she was cold. She was shaking like a river-dipper.

'*The man is here*' she said '*the robed man in brown, the man I've always seen.*'

'*What tosh, can't you ever relax? Can't you enjoy yourself?*'

'*He won't leave me alone. He . . . he knows me. Please, I'm frightened and I want to go home.*'

Delia was quivering and pale and her skin was mottled with goose bumps. She looked really quite dramatically the less pretty sister, more than usual.

'*Stop being so odd, Delia. It makes you very difficult to love.*'

I was dancing and sweating, then I was canoodling with the racing driver.

'*Plug one in for me old boy!*' said a famous actor, and we all roared with laughter.

I wander back up to the domed entrance hall in case the man from English Heritage is waiting, but there's nobody. The door is closed. Did I close the door?

'Hello?'

I sit down in an armchair in the drawing room that says 'Please do not sit'. I've paid my membership fees for years and I've been rudely stood up, so I shall jolly well sit down. I swear I can hear music somewhere. It is my mind playing tricks on me. I call out feebly 'Is there someone here?'

There is a scratching noise in the walls but it's the same with any old house, heaving and adjusting. Creaking. Hundreds of years of history leaking out. Perfectly normal.

I remember we all went and saw the infamous pet lemur, which was not biting people or cuddling its mistress as the legends have it, but snoozing in a fetid heap.

'Well bugger that, Mah-Jongg you party pooper' said a shiny Frenchman in plus fours, and we all roared with laughter.

Then Delia was with me again, pulling at my sleeve, and I followed her.

We crept into Virginia's boudoir. I was terribly drunk. There were people lounging on the floor, on cushions, smoking. We both gazed at the leather map. It buzzed. Hidden machinery behind the walls. Eltham the electric toy.
'I told you this place was haunted' she said.
'Did you?'
'Are you drunk?'
'Absomagnificat' I said, and giggled.

She whispered.

He knows me! He said he used to watch over me as a child, while I was sleeping. He described the inside of my bedroom. He said he liked my paintings, he said I have to paint my pictures for him.'

She pointed to the curtain in the corner of the boudoir.

'Through there in the map room, but it's terribly secret. He's very angry with me.'

I remember she was multiplying in front of my eyes.

Two Delias, each a babbling frenzy about the blasted man and his paintings.

Three Delias, frightened, pale and dim.

I did my best impression of our poor departed father. I looked at Delia and, swaying, said *'Nobody cares for your made-up terrors.'*

And then I was whooping, riding on my pilot's shoulders across the lawn to the glasshouses to see Stephen Courtauld's world-famous orchids.

Sometime in the very early morning Delia was on the lawn and she looked luminously white and I wrapped her in someone's shawl.

'I don't know what to do' she said. *'He's come for me. I have to go with him.'*

She gazed into my eyes and she said to me, *'Will you come and find me? Please come and find me.'*

I was so sloshed. I don't know what I said to her.

I suppose I was unkind.
I suppose I said *'Absolute nonsense.'*

Eltham loomed out of the dark, sparkling and noisy, like a huge electric ship made of jewels and I watched my strange little sister step back inside it.

✢

I shift uncomfortably on the chair in the drawing room. I do not feel safe in this house. It's the memories. All the people I was here with are presumably dead and gone. It's just me in Eltham Palace with my memories. Nasty me, in 1937, surrounded by glitz. Nasty me, now, all alone.

Sometime in the early morning I was wrapped in the pilot's jacket and there was a man playing the clarinet, and someone gave me a shot of herbal liqueur out of a tiny crystal glass and we all bundled into cars and someone said my sister had left, and then she wasn't at home, and then sometime later we phoned the exchange and got through to Eltham and they told us that no guests were left at the house, and then in a shambolic and slightly embarrassed manner we phoned the police.

They searched for her, and I was asked a million times about the party, and I couldn't remember much, and my head hurt so terribly for those first days that I simply sobbed and repeated that it had been awfully noisy and my sister had met a chap in a brown costume.

They dredged the moat and searched the Tudor sewers. They stopped a fellow in a field who was in some kind of monk's robe, Eric Gill get-up, but he turned out to be a genuine eccentric who had never set foot in the palace.

Delia was simply gone.

Society Daughter Disappears at Eltham.

Mother never got well. On the evening after the party, before we really understood Delia was properly missing, she had a nightmare about Eltham. She said she dreamed that Delia was trapped between the old bits and the new bits of the palace. Lost. She saw her face in a painting. She raved and shrieked about her daughter being imprisoned in Eltham. On her deathbed she said *'Find your sister'* and I never even tried. I never bloody tried.

I never came back to Eltham until today.

I heave myself off the armchair and wander back through the entrance hall, swiping at the fusty air with my stick.

I can smell some kind of chemical or medical odour. Girlhood smells. Particles of the young me. Nostalgia.

I go through into the green servants' corridor and turn left down into the basement. I'm very frail these days. One step at a time. Descending past the shadow of the younger me on these same stairs.
I never went to another party at Eltham. I married a Scot and fled the flat Home Counties. I became a dull, wealthy, landowning wife of a laird. I've got dozens of grandchildren who sometimes phone and thank me for money.
My husband said I was a fragile flower. I said he was an ox. Flowers outlive oxen you know.

The Courtaulds ditched Eltham when one too many bombs landed on the great hall which they had so tirelessly faked back into authenticity. They eventually settled in Southern Rhodesia and presumably lived out their days reminiscing about the razzle-dazzle of this place.

The basement is painted red like animal innards. I swear I can hear music.

'Oh! Bloody hell!' I yelp, because there is a mannequin dressed up as an air-raid warden. I whack it crossly with my stick.
'Piss off' I say to it, in passing.
My poor ancient heart jangles in its cage. I detest shocks.
I tiptoe through to the billiards room. My pulse is plunking in my ears, making me nervous.
It's warm down here and I feel agitated.

There it is, the Italianate mural. As incongruous now as it was then. Pastiche. An Umbrian soap advert clinging to the wall for dear life.
Is this what my mother dreamed of? She must've seen this mural at a party.
I peer at the painting. There are two girls, carrying bowls on their heads.
I'm suddenly desperately disconcerted and confused. This place is making me ill.
There are tears in my eyes. 'Delia?' I speak to the servant girl. For heaven's sake, it doesn't look a thing like Delia.
I feel terribly, abjectly alone. I want my husband. I want Delia. I was a terrible sister. Sniffling, I lean my head against the mural and whisper,

'I'm sorry I was so relentlessly cruel. Forgive me, Delia.'

A hand claps down on my shoulder.

I scream.
I flail, spin around, waggle my stick and topple back against the mural.

There is a little man in a brown suit.

'There, there ma'am' he says 'it's just a pretty picture.'

The shock has rendered me completely speechless. I am close to losing control of my antique bladder. I am trying to catch my breath.

He simply stares at me and says it again in his strange vinegary voice; 'Just a pretty picture.'

My hands are shaking quite ridiculously. I brandish my stick at him.

'You're late!' I snap.

'Well, you seem to know your way around. Welcome back.'

'Welcome back?'

He has peculiar round eyes, the little English Heritage man. Eyes like little electric light bulbs, glowing gold. His face puts me in mind of the bloody awful lemur. I glance at the portrait of the pet in the mural beside me. Yes, he has a look of Mah-Jongg, this little man. That's probably why they hired him.

'Yes, I assume you've been to Eltham before, since you know your way around?'

'I have, many years ago, yes. Anyway, I was rather hoping to see the leather map, in Virginia's boudoir.'

'Follow me, ma'am.'

He goes in front and I follow him slowly up. My pulse rate is still preposterously high and the thought crosses my mind that a shock like that, at my age, might have killed me. I think to myself that not only will I be cancelling my membership but I shall be writing a strongly worded letter of complaint to English Heritage. I despise being given a fright.

I am about to voice my upset when I realise the little man is mumbling something.

He is issuing forth a peculiar stream of unrelated and half-formed titbits of Eltham trivia, some of which strike me as complete nonsense.

'They say the ghost of Thomas Wolsey appears, some-times, and you can actually hear the marble bust of Virginia Courtauld cry out in shock, some say she's alive at night, and up here in the servant quarter is where Erasmus might have sat in deep conversation with the courtiers of . . .'

'Well, thank you, but I think I'll be fine without the folk-lore and hearsay.'

We walk across the entrance hall and down towards Virginia's boudoir. The little man fidgets with his pockets. He squirms and judders as if there are fleas in his suit. He smells strongly of iodine and the smell makes me feel . . . vulnerable. I haven't smelt iodine in years.

'Here we are, ma'am.'

I don't feel well. The fright he caused me in the base-ment has given me a tightness in the chest. My breaths are shallow.

There's jazz music playing and I feel hot and stifled. My bones are aching and I don't like this peculiar little man.

'Where is that music coming from?'

'Music, ma'am?'
And he's right, there isn't any music playing.
I'm flustered, that's all.

'Here on the wall you see the famous leather map, complete
with the—'
'How long have you worked at Eltham?' I interrupt him.
'Oh, a long time. I've always been here really. Now ma'am, I
see your gaze drifts to the velvet curtain there in the corner.
Would you like to see the map room?'

He says 'map room' softly and with an especially repellent
twist of his little simian face.

'Don't worry, I think I shall leave now, actually, I have a
taxi b—'

'YOU CAN'T' he shrieks and squirms his hands around
in his pockets. 'I mean, you must see the map room, there
are paintings on the wall, only recently discovered, dating
from the 1930s. It's one of the most remarkable rooms at
Eltham Palace.'

My stomach wobbles.

'Paintings?'

'Come, come, ma'am' he says and holds back the curtain. 'You're going to enjoy this.'

I step through.

It's a small room with stained and torn maps on all the walls. Around the maps there are little painted motifs. A funny Irish man in a green suit. Coral, jewels, some faint airplanes, palm trees, camels and a thorny green dragon. My mouth is atrociously dry and I feel perhaps I am about to vomit. I realise with abject surety as I gaze upon them that these are my sister's paintings. That is Delia's sweet signature Britannia with a shield, the same Britannia she did on letterheads. I would know her curious style anywhere. My sister did these paintings, but how? And when? The night of the party? My brain skitters and leaps. I don't know what to think. I fear I must be having some kind of emotion-induced hallucination. I am about to ask the guide when I notice something. Above the European map there are two young women depicted, together, in frocks. One is slender and beautiful, with flowing red hair, she is flushed and grinning. The other is shorter, and plumper, less pretty, and she looks terrified. She is grimacing and pointing across the top of the map.

'You're going to be joining Delia' says the little man, behind me.

'What did you just say?' I spin about and face him.

'I said, "You're going to enjoy the detail there."'

I am so lightheaded I don't really understand what is happening. I turn back to look at the paintings and I support myself with one shaking hand on the wall.

What is that? On the wall. Bloody hell what in god's name . . .

I can scarcely believe my eyes, but the taller girl is paler than she was just seconds ago. She looks less confident. The painting is changing. I am unwell, surely. I keep on looking. The other less pretty lady is open-mouthed, blazing with intent, pointing along the top of the map. I follow her outstretched arm and there, perched on the end of the map, is a little man in brown robes, with a face like a lemur.

SCREEEEAAACHH!; from behind me a vicious explosion of noise.

I turn around brandishing my pathetic stick and the man leaps and he *is* the lemur, the hideous Mah-Jongg, orange eyes glazed with rage, swivelling and spinning in their sockets, rows of sharp teeth all the way back into his black throat, and I start to scream and he leaps at me and knocks me back against the wall, punching me hard in the chest with two paw-like fists. I struggle against him, lashing out, and he bites my hand, like a dozen pins driven into my skin, and the pain is simply unbelievable. I howl. The shock of being attacked is atrocious, but the sheer surprise of the violence merges with appalling incredulity because as I have met the wall I have not stopped. The wall is soft. It seems to be absorbing me. I feel a gradual tug, then a stronger pull and I can't get my weight forward, I am shouting quite insanely now, yelping, gasping 'Oh GOD' terrified spitting gasps of panic 'HELP ME!' dribbling bursts of sobs, I am not strong enough, I am going to drown, the wall seems to be pulling me in, the lemur man has gone, and something is snarling and tugging at me from behind now, hissing, growling, pulling me into the wall, I kick and scramble and claw at the air, but all is liquid and the room is dark and I can't hold on and then all of a sudden through my wailing there is a familiar voice, a young woman's voice and she is saying 'No', she is angry and determined and she is saying 'No NO!' and I join her frantic calls and I start yelling 'No. Please, No!' and I feel two hands on my shoulders pushing me forward, strong but small hands, pushing me back out of the wall, out into the room and I call out in pain and confusion 'Delia? DELIA?!' and there is a hard two-handed thump of a final shove on my shoulders and I spill out onto the floor in a heap and pass beyond the nightmare into total dreadful collapse.

✦

Dear Mr Porter,

Thank you for your letter.
I no longer work for English Heritage but yes I do remember Mrs Charbury.
This was 2012. I was meant to show her around. I found her on the front drive, in a terrible state. She said her sister Delia was trapped in some paintings in the map room and had been since 1937. She said the lemur had attacked her. I admit to you I thought it was nonsense. I thought she was crackers. For starters the palace was locked and alarmed.

I opened up after Mrs Charbury had left in the ambulance. There was nobody there. I called out the name Delia several times, because I had promised Mrs Charbury I would. I was embarrassed, and a little unnerved, alone in there calling out for someone. The map room was closed with no sign of any disturbance.

I searched the premises thoroughly. You ask about a
bad feeling in there. Yes, I did have a bad feeling in
there, that day. The only noteworthy thing was that
one of the WW2 educational costumes from the basement, a brown woollen suit, had been left upstairs in
the Mah-Jongg Suite, presumably by one of the half-
term school parties. And that was that.

In 2014 when the restorers uncovered the paintings
in the map room I admit I was highly perturbed and
remembered Mrs Charbury's terrified ramblings about
her sister. I attempted to make contact, but she had
cancelled her English Heritage membership. I found
her with a bit of googling and saw that she passed
away back in 2012, after her visit to Eltham. Poor old
dear, she died of an infected animal bite to her hand.
Nasty business.
Anyway, strange old place, Eltham.
Good luck with your story,

Rory Kippax.

AFTERWORDS

WITHIN THESE WALLS

How the Castles, Abbeys and Houses of
England Inspired the Ghost Story

Andrew Martin

The ruins of Minster Lovell Hall – an elegant Oxfordshire manor house of the fifteenth century – are promisingly located for the ghost fancier, lying between the graveyard of St Kenelm's church and a lonely stretch of the River Windrush. The English Heritage noticeboard announces that the site is open at 'any reasonable daylight hour', which possibly does not include dusk on a day of heavy rain. But those were the conditions as I stood alone before the manor, thinking of the rumoured discovery of a skeleton in the basement in 1718, supposedly the body of Francis Lovell who had hidden there after the Battle of Stoke in 1487, at the end of the Wars of the Roses, and died of starvation. All around me were sounds, some explicable (the cooing of doves roosting in the remains of the tower, the rushing of the Windrush), some less so. Suddenly, there was a great, grey shape over my head. I looked up and saw a bird – a heron, I think – coasting to land on the adjacent pond.

If I had run away without looking up, I would have had a ghost story. As I walked back to the house in which I was staying, I contemplated developing one anyway, just to see the effect of saying to my hostess, 'I saw a ghost just now at Minster Lovell Hall . . .' I would have felt the lie justified by the entertainment value, and it is possible that I would have forgotten that I was lying the moment I began the story. If I had told it well enough, my story might have been passed on by my hostess. She might have embellished it – consciously or unconsciously – in her turn, and each of these retellings would have been a tribute to the lure of the Minster Lovell ruins.

The dissemination of my tale would have been rather folkloric, in that it would have been communicated by word of mouth, with no undue fussiness about the facts. Since the late eighteenth century, we have kept our works of fiction and non-fiction on separate shelves, but a ghost story should always *seem to be* non-fiction or – to use the word favoured by the late Victorian investigators of the Society for Psychical Research – 'veridical'.

Often, a tale's truthfulness is insisted on at the outset. Here is the title of what has been called, because of its forensic tone, the first modern ghost story: 'A true Relation of the Apparition of one Mrs Veal the next day after her death to one Mrs Bargrave, at Canterbury, the eight of September, 1705'. The story, by Daniel Defoe, begins:

This thing is so rare in all its circumstances, and on so good authority, that my reading and conversation has not given me anything like it. It is fit to gratify the most ingenious and serious inquirer. Mrs Bargrave is the person to whom Mrs Veal appeared after her death; she is my intimate friend, and I can avouch for her reputation these past fifteen or sixteen years . . .

This presentation of credentials would become a familiar device and is used by Oscar Wilde in his parody 'The Canterville Ghost' (1887). As Lord Canterville says: 'I feel bound to tell you, Mr Otis, that the ghost has been seen by several living members of my family, as well as by the rector of the parish, the Reverend Augustus Dampier, who is a fellow of King's College, Cambridge.'

Whether nominally factual or fictional, ghosts tend to fit standard templates. By the nineteenth century, Charles Dickens could write that they are 'reducible to a very few general types and classes; for, ghosts have little originality and "walk" in a beaten track'. These words come from the mouth of the elderly and irritatingly sagacious narrator of 'A Christmas Tree' (1850), a minor Dickens' ghost story. Such ghost world-weariness doesn't belong to Dickens himself, who stated, 'I have always had a strong interest in the subject and never knowingly lose an opportunity of pursuing it.' But most ghosts *are* conventional in their appearance and behaviour, either because that is just what they are like, or because that is what most people who talk about them are like.

The female ghosts of castles or big houses, for example, tend to be 'ladies' and they tend to be white. White ladies have been spotted at (among others) Beeston Castle in Cheshire, Rochester Castle, Kent and Goodrich Castle,

Herefordshire. Wistful aristocratic ladies are also available in green (Helmsley Castle, Yorkshire) and blue (Berry Pomeroy Castle in Devon, commonly regarded as English Heritage's most haunted site, and also in possession of a white one).

Headlessness is another common complaint among ghosts. That icon of decapitation, Sir Walter Raleigh, appears at Sherborne Old Castle in Dorset and a headless drummer drums at Dover Castle. In the vicinity of Okehampton Castle in Devon, Lady Mary Howard (b. 1596) rides in a coach made from the bones of her four dead husbands, daintily decorated with a skull on every corner, and driven by a headless coachman. At dawn on old Christmas Day (about 6 January), a coach pulled by headless horses races through the ruins of Whitby Abbey and over the cliff edge – which makes me appreciate my computer's point when it keeps changing 'headless' into 'heedless'.

We cannot leave the stock spirits without mentioning ghostly monks. There is one or more at Waverley Abbey in Surrey, at Bayham Abbey and Reculver Towers in Kent, at Thetford and Binham Priories in Norfolk, at Hardwick Old Hall in Derbyshire, Rufford Abbey in Nottinghamshire, Thornton Abbey in Lincolnshire, at Roche Abbey and Conisbrough Castle, both in South Yorkshire, and Whalley Abbey in Lancashire.

A historical digression is required here, in order to note that monks – as the principal chroniclers of medieval life – were also among the first ghost story writers. In about 1400, for example, a monk at the great Cistercian abbey of

Byland in North Yorkshire transcribed twelve ghost stories in the spare pages at the end of a popular encyclopaedia, the *Elucidarium* (so called because it shed light on points of theology and folk belief). The anonymous ghost story collector had the concern with provenance that we have already noted. He was careful in his scene setting – mentioning many places in the locality – and he gives the name of the protagonists in over half of the stories. The second tale, for example, concerns 'a miraculous struggle between a spirit and a man who lived in the time of Richard II' – a tailor called Snowball who encountered the ghost on his way home to Ampleforth, which is very near to Byland.

One ghost took the form of a disembodied voice shouting 'How, how, how' at midnight near a crossroads. It then turned into a pale horse, and when the percipient (William de Bradeforth) charged 'the spirit in the name of the Lord and by the power of the blood of Jesus Christ to depart', it withdrew 'like a piece of canvas unfurling its four corners and billowing away'. In other stories, the spirit is more corporeal, a revenant of the kind associated with Scandinavian folklore: a lumbering animated corpse. In the third story, the revenant – the spirit of a man called Robert from nearby Kilburn, who has been frightening the locals and making the dogs bark loudly – is captured in a graveyard and pinioned on the church stile, whereupon it, or he, begins to speak 'not with his tongue but from deep within his innards, as if from an empty barrel'. The story ends, as do most of the Byland ghost stories, and many others chronicled by monks throughout the

Middle Ages, with the victim/protagonist confessing his sins and being given absolution. The monks did tend to conclude their stories in this way, stressing the efficacy of prayer in releasing souls from purgatory.

Even after the suppression of the monasteries, Catholics continued to believe in this pre-Reformation type of ghost: a soul returning and requesting prayers. Given that Protestantism had dispensed with the notion of purgatory, anyone holding such beliefs began to seem primitive and superstitious. Hence the sinister monks populating Gothic fiction, the genre that directly preceded the modern ghost story.

Gothic fiction (a romantic backlash against a dominant neo-classicism) had its lurid heyday in the late eighteenth century. It promoted the antique, the violent and the macabre. The spectral monks (as well as the white ladies and ranks of the headless) associated with so many English Heritage properties were probably instituted during this Gothic phase, monastics seeming to epitomise the decadence and hypocrisy of the medieval world that had brought their monasteries to ruin. Matthew Gregory Lewis set the template with *The Monk* (1796), closely followed by such sensational works as *The Italian or the Confessional of the Black Penitents* (1797) by Ann Radcliffe, *Gondez the Monk* (1805) by William Henry Ireland and *Melmoth the Wanderer* (1820) by Charles Maturin.

This anti-Catholic strain can perhaps still be detected in the work of the distinguished antiquarian and ghost story writer M.R. James, especially in the diabolism of the eponymous 'Count Magnus' (1904). (It was James, incidentally, who first transcribed and published the Byland stories – *transcribed*, not translated; he enjoyed the 'very refreshing' Latin in which they were written.)

The Gothic writers were drawn towards monks not only because of their exotic theology, but also because they were so picturesquely accommodated. Gothic literature got its name, after all – from its association with medieval 'Gothic' buildings and ruins, from the monasteries and castles with their underground passages, brooding battlements and crumbling staircases. Its level of hysteria was unsustainable, however, and its energy was channelled, and the sinister backdrops tamed, in the more decorous historical romances of Walter Scott. The new sensationalism resided in ghost stories, whose authors tried to throw off the materialism implied by Darwinism, just as the Gothic writers rebelled against eighteenth-century rationalism.

It is arguable that ghost stories were the first form of 'genre fiction', and for a while scientific advances complemented, rather than negated, ghostliness. There is an analogy to be drawn, for example, between telegraphy and telepathy. These new ghosts went at large into the world, and the familiar stage sets – ruined castles or monasteries – were no longer required . . .

Ghosts migrated to residential areas, where captive audiences awaited. The dining room of almost any Victorian house might have accommodated a séance, whose genteel sitters were not expecting a galumphing Frankenstein-ian revenant of medieval ghost stories to pitch up. There was not sufficient faith to animate such a creature. It was accepted that the afterlife would be proved obliquely, by a disembodied voice, a drop in temperature, a movement of the planchette. If the sitters did manage to conjure up a manifestation, it would be fleeting and transparent.

Ghost hunting became increasingly domesticated, concerned with faces at the window, slamming doors, creaking floorboards, and scufflings behind the skirting board. (In Victorian and Edwardian ghost stories, the naive principals would at first attribute these noises to rats, but rats were not so lightly invoked after they had played their role in the horrors of the First World War trenches.) A classic of the haunted house genre is Sheridan Le Fanu's story of 1851, 'An Account of Some Strange Disturbances in Aungier Street'. In this story – the brilliance of which is suggested by the title alone (the gloominess of 'Aungier') – two Dublin students rent a house that had belonged to a hanging judge. Lying in bed one night, one of the young men becomes aware of 'a sort of horrid but undefined preparation going forward in some unknown quarter . . .' Le Fanu himself would be kept awake at night with horrible imaginings. He had a persistent nightmare of a large house collapsing on him as he slept, and when he died in bed – of a heart attack and with a shocked expression on his face – his doctor observed, 'That house fell at last!'

A bed is also the focal point of one of the best M.R. James ghost stories, 'Oh Whistle, and I'll Come to You, My Lad' (1904). The ghostliness starts out of doors. A very rationalist academic called Parkins is walking along a bleak, grey beach in Suffolk. He comes to the site of a Templar preceptory, where he unearths a bone whistle. He takes it back to the inn where he is lodging, and into his bedroom, where he rashly blows it, causing a wind to stir beyond the windows. It is in the bedroom that the manifestation finally occurs, in the form of crumpled bed linen – never to be forgotten by anyone who has seen Jonathan Miller's short film of the story, broadcast in 1968. My reading of this denouement is that the 'sincere and humourless' Parkins suffers a twofold comeuppance. First, there is the manifestation. Secondly, he is reduced to trembling fear by such a bathetic object as a bedsheet.

The most famous of all domestic hauntings was chronicled by the celebrated ghost hunter and charlatan, Harry Price, in his book of 1940, *The Most Haunted House in England* – namely Borley Rectory in Essex. When he repaired to Borley, which he did regularly over ten years, Price carried his 'ghost hunter's kit', which included a flask of brandy (in case anybody fainted), and a pair of 'felt overshoes used for creeping unheard about the house in order that neither human beings nor paranormal "entities" shall be disturbed when producing "phenomena".' Here, you feel, is the ghost hunter as lounge lizard.

Any sort of house might be haunted. Dickens spoke of the 'avoided house', the neglected and mysterious property that is put to shame by (or possibly shames) the primness of the conventional dwellings on either side. In literature, haunted houses do tend to be at the upper end of the market. In Walter de la Mare's story, 'Out of the Deep' (1923), the protagonist, Jimmie, inherits his uncle's 'horrible old London mansion'. In 'Moonlight Sonata' (1931) by Alexander Woollcott one of the two principals inhabits 'the collapsing family manor house to which he had indignantly fallen heir'. Then again, poltergeists do not need a large, grand house. They will turn up anywhere there is furniture to throw about.

'Haunted Houses', a poem of 1858 by Henry Wadsworth Longfellow, begins:

> All houses in which men have lived and died
> Are haunted houses . . .

And the more deaths the better, frankly, which is why I went to Minster Lovell Hall at dusk. It is what takes me to any English Heritage property: as the more studious visitors are in the next room hearing about the dentilled cornice and door surrounds, I am lingering in the previous room, and staring into the clouded mirror, daring any face from the past to appear alongside my own.

I am hoping, in short, for the sight of a ghost, and the sense of wonderment that would – I am confident – accompany the jolt of pure fear.

A GAZETTEER OF
ENGLISH HERITAGE HAUNTINGS

Ghosts have been seen – or felt – at English Heritage sites the length and breadth of the country. Here is a nationwide selection – by no means exhaustive – of properties which are said to be haunted and the shuddering histories behind them, including the eight locations which inspired the stories in this book.

London

Eltham Palace and Gardens

This opulent palace, which at its peak far exceeded the size of Hampton Court, began life as the manor of Bishop Odo of Bayeux, half-brother of William the Conqueror. In 1296 Bishop Antony Bek of Durham built a manor house, parts of which have been excavated, and in the early fourteenth century Edward II gave this moated manor to his wife. It became a favourite royal residence and was greatly enlarged. The great hall seen today was built by Edward IV in the 1470s, a magnificent space for the king to entertain up to 2,000 guests, as he did in 1482. Henry VIII spent much of his boyhood at Eltham, but under Elizabeth I the palace began to fall into ruin. It wasn't until 1933 that it was returned to a state of splendour, when the fashionable couple Stephen and Virginia (Ginie) Courtauld leased the estate from the Crown. Stephen was enormously rich – having inherited wealth enough from his family's textile business to live at leisure, pursuing cultural and philanthropic interests. While preserving the medieval hall, he and Ginie employed the architects Sealy and Paget to build a new home, fitted with every technological convenience: a glamorous, ultra-modern setting for their collections of art and furniture, and their regular parties.

Ginie had a much-adored pet lemur named Mah-Jongg who was infamous for biting people he did not like. Mah-Jongg had his own heated and designer-decorated sleeping quarters at Eltham which can be seen today. The leather map of the estate mentioned in Max Porter's story was created for the Courtaulds and remains above the fireplace in the boudoir. The vignettes he describes are in the neighbouring map room, where conservators have recently uncovered (beneath later wallpaper) large maps of areas to which the Courtaulds travelled pasted to the walls. The vignettes were painted onto the walls adjacent the maps, depicting scenes and characters from around the world.

But the most famous ghost of Eltham is reputedly one of the palace tour guides, who was deeply attached to the place and died only a week after retiring. He has been seen subsequently, conducting tours when the house is meant to be shut. Staff report numerous other incidents, so frequent that, when asked, one laughed at the suggestion that this must be disturbing and declared that they get used to it: the low voices and footsteps heard when locking up the house at night, and the mysterious locking or unlocking of doors. This happens regularly on the minstrels' gallery above the great hall and in one of the adjoining bedrooms used by Ginie's nephews.

Another intriguing report is that of a woman in medieval dress who has been seen a few times by security guards at night. She has been observed walking through the arches of the passage at the end of the great hall, through the cupboards that now conceal the arches and the modern electrics which are installed there.

Chiswick House and Gardens

Chiswick House is one of the most significant – and enchanting – examples of eighteenth-century British architecture. It was designed and built by the 3rd Earl of Burlington in the 1720s, a pioneer work of neo-classical architecture inspired by the sixteenth-century Italian architect Andrea Palladio and by the villas, temples and palaces of ancient Rome. The ornate interiors and formal gardens were created by Burlington and the architect, painter and garden designer William Kent.

The gardens were restored during a major project in 2010. Earlier conservation work, in 1958, seems to have restored something rather different – the cook. Workmen began to smell frying bacon in an area that once housed the kitchens. The men put it down to a ghostly cook – apparently still bent on duties at the kitchen range.

Jewel Tower

Nestling discreetly between the Houses of Parliament and Westminster Abbey, the tower is a precious survivor of the medieval Palace of Westminster. The Jewel Tower was built in 1365 by Edward III at the south-west corner of his palace, beside his private apartments and garden. It was intended to house his personal collection of jewels, gold and silver.

In the 1950s excavation of the moat turned up various objects, among them, most curiously, two heads: one of a man and one of a cat. The cat was of especial interest as her skull had been skinned and painted green. Superstition? A witch's familiar? But it is neither man nor cat that seems to haunt the tower, although the cat's skull is on display. A woman has been seen to walk through the wall into the tower courtyard, dressed in the fashion of the seventeenth century – at which time there had indeed been a door in the wall to the courtyard.

Kenwood

This magnificent house, triumphantly restored, stands on the edge of Hampstead Heath in parkland landscaped by Humphry Repton. Kenwood was remodelled by Robert Adam between 1764 and 1779 for William Murray, 1st Earl of Mansfield, and contains some of Adam's finest surviving interiors. In 1925 Kenwood was bought by Edward

Cecil Guinness, 1st Earl of Iveagh, and subsequently left by him to the nation, together with an outstanding collection of Old Master and British paintings, including works by Rembrandt, Vermeer, Turner, Reynolds, Gainsborough, Constable and Romney.

In the upper hall, off the great stair, are the dazzling full-length portraits from the Suffolk Collection. Here, with no one but a room attendant present, the door has been known to slam shut with some violence. Some suggest it could be the ghost of one of Kenwood's most famous residents, Dido Elizabeth Belle, the mixed-race great-niece of Lord Mansfield.

The South East

Dover Castle, Kent

Dover Castle stands high on the White Cliffs above the English Channel at the narrowest crossing point between England and France. It has seen unbroken active service from its first building under William the Conqueror after the Battle of Hastings in 1066 until the Cold War. In 1216 it withstood one of the most terrible medieval English sieges, after which a remarkable series of new defences was built, linked together by underground tunnels, and enlarged and extended in the eighteenth and nineteenth centuries.

In 1797, during the Napoleonic Wars, a new series of tunnels was excavated within the famous white cliffs themselves to accommodate the large number of troops needed to man the defences. During the Second World War these tunnels housed the command centre that controlled naval operations in the Channel, and it was from here that in May 1940 the 'miracle' of Dunkirk was planned and coordinated – resulting in the evacuation of 338,000 Allied troops from the coast of France.

Dover has sheltered many thousands of lives within its walls over its long history. It is no wonder ghost stories abound. In the great tower, the lower half of a man's body was seen by two members of staff in the doorway to the King's chamber. Another staff member, while cleaning the basement, saw the figure of a Cavalier, and another has seen the figure of a woman in a red dress on the stairs and along the mural gallery. There are no stories attached to any of the ghosts at Dover, except for that of a drummer boy: it is said that the boy was carrying a sum of money on an errand to the castle and was attacked and decapitated. There have been numerous reports of the beat of his drum near the castle battlements.

Although there are no recorded reports of an American airman, such as in Stuart Evers' story, the ghosts of naval officers have been seen in the castle's wartime tunnels. Here, too, there are regular reports by staff and visitors of slamming doors, footsteps and voices, as well as one curious sighting of a seventeenth-century pikeman. An American couple commented to staff on the very realistic cries and moans of the audio recreation within the tunnels, but there was no such recreation then in place.

Intrigued by the frequency of all these phenomena, in 1991 a team of investigators visited Dover Castle, recording various events, the most remarkable being a pair of shaking doors in the great tower's stairwell, which was caught on video tape – the footage was later shown on the television series *Strange but True?*. There is another oddity. During the filming of this episode a psychic was called in. He was 'given the name Helen' while standing in the wartime tunnels' repeater room – reportedly the most haunted of the castle. A few days later an Australian tourist said she had seen a man in the tunnels who seemed distressed, and asked her 'where Helen was'. Years later, during an exercise in the tunnels on a school trip, a boy drew a figure with a speech bubble: 'Where is Helen?' – the question asked him, he told staff, by a man he had met in the tunnels.

Medieval Merchant's House, Southampton, Hampshire

This house was built in about 1290 for a wine merchant, one John Fortin, and stands on what was one of the busiest streets of medieval Southampton near the town wall. Southampton had developed into a large and prosperous port, grown rich on Continental trade. Fortin's house included a cellar where he could store his wine, a shop at the front of the ground floor, and a bed chamber which was jettied out over the street below.

The house has been restored to its appearance in the mid-fourteenth century, including the cellar. Some years ago, staff raked over the cellar floor, which was then covered with gravel, before leaving and locking up for the day. The following morning they were astonished to see a set a footprints clearly visible in the gravel. The footprints started in the middle of the room and disappeared into a wall – the last one only partly visible, as if the ghostly tread had walked on through the stones.

Netley Abbey, Hampshire

The ruins of Netley Abbey form the most complete survival of a Cistercian monastery in southern England. The abbey was founded in 1238 by the powerful Peter des Roches, Bishop of Winchester, and after the Suppression was granted by Henry VIII to Sir William Paulet, his treasurer, who converted the abbey into a mansion house. But in 1704 the house was sold for building materials. The remainder gradually fell into ruin, its state of romantic neglect by the end of the eighteenth century inspiring many a Gothic writer and Romantic spirit.

One of the many ghosts reported at Netley is said to be the man to whom the house was sold for building materials in 1704 – a Southampton builder named Walter Taylor. Having signed the contract, Taylor dreamed that a stone from one of the church windows fell upon his head and killed him. He consulted a friend about the dream, afraid that it was a warning, but in the end decided to go ahead with the demolition. While at work at the east end of the abandoned church a stone from a window arch fell on his head, fractured his skull and killed him.

Portchester Castle, Hampshire

Portchester Castle, at the north end of Portsmouth Harbour, is set within the imposing walls of a Roman 'Saxon shore' fort – the most complete example in northern Europe. During Norman rule a keep was built, turning the shore fort into a castle, which was expanded and modernised throughout the Middle Ages. It remained a residence into the seventeenth century and was used to house prisoners during the Napoleonic Wars. The last of these prisoners left in 1819.

Given its long and varied history, it is not surprising that Portchester's ghosts are similarly varied – a monk who wanders the bank along the outer wall (an Augustinian priory was founded here in the twelfth century), a Roman centurion who stands guard at the gatehouse and a Victorian woman in white. On one occasion a member of staff and a visitor witnessed a horse gallop across the inner bailey ward. It might have been mistaken for a living creature, had not the horse emerged from the castle walls and simply disappeared across the bailey.

Upnor Castle, Kent

Upnor Castle was built by order of Elizabeth I in 1559 on the bank of the River Medway to defend the royal fleet and new dockyard developing near the village of Chatham, just a little upstream. It was enlarged at the end of the sixteenth century and in 1667 the brave efforts of its garrison helped prevent Dutch warships from reaching and destroying Chatham during their otherwise victorious raid on the Medway. The castle then became a powder magazine to supply the Navy and a series of new defences being built along the river. By 1691 Upnor had become its largest gunpowder store. To protect this cache of explosives a small company of soldiers was employed and soon after 1718 was housed in the new barracks – one of the earliest in the country.

'Ghost truths, not ghost stories' is how one present-day member of staff describes the situation at Upnor. There is a list of usual occurences. This staff member, sweeping up before closing time, saw a boy in Georgian clothes standing outside the barracks, holding out his hand as if passing a message at the door. He vanished after a minute or so. More disturbingly, a face appeared over another member of staff's shoulder in the gatehouse – a man with straggly, shoulder length hair, about forty years old. But it is the shop in the barracks that causes the most trouble. Here staff have seen handfuls of leaflets thrown to the floor in front of their eyes, and found, on opening up in the morning, boxes of merchandise hurled across the room, their contents scattered. Once – less petulantly, it seems – a basket of toy rings, with the pirate's skull and crossbones, had been turned upside down on the shop counter, the basket placed neatly over the top.

Tilbury Fort, Essex

This coastal fort on the Thames estuary is the finest example of a seventeenth-century bastioned fortress in England, with its complete circuit of moats and outworks still substantially surviving. It was begun in 1670, under Charles II, on the site of an earlier fort built by Henry VIII, and was designed to stop warships sailing upriver and its garrison equipped to prevent land attack. In 1716 two powder magazines were built to store vast quantities of gunpowder destined for the government forces of the emerging Empire. Scottish prisoners were held here after the Jacobite Rising of 1745 and much later the fort's modern guns helped shoot down a raiding Zeppelin during the First World War.

A diary is held at the fort that belonged to one James Bowley who joined the army in 1838. In it he describes an event on the Thames after the Royal Engineers were sent to clear a brig, *The William*, that had been hit by a paddle steamer and caught in the shipping lanes of the Thames. The Engineers sank a chest of explosives beneath it to blow it up into removable pieces but one of the men, Corporal Henry Mitchell, became caught during the operation. He was wearing the heavy, cumbersome diving gear of the time and his oxygen pipe became entangled. He did not surface in time and the brig blew, people unknowingly cheering on the riverside. Mitchell was found among the debris and brought to the surgeon at the fort, but nothing could be done. The figure of this unfortunate young man is said to haunt the fort where he died.

A man's mumbling voice and his footsteps are also some-times heard in the chapel – believed to be the ghost of a former chaplain. Redcoat soldiers have been reported march-ing by the blast walls as well as other sundry voices of both men and women.

The South West

Pendennis Castle, Cornwall

This Tudor fortress, together with its twin, St Mawes, stands near Falmouth, at the entrance to the Carrick Roads, the huge natural harbour at the mouth of the River Fal. The two castles face each other across a mile of sea, where for more than 400 years their guns pointed south to the open Channel, and inwards, barring access to the river. They were built in the 1540s as part of Henry VIII's sweeping pro-gramme of defence, amid the national fear of invasion from the Catholic powers of Europe. The danger passed, but the fortresses remained armed until 1956, playing an active role in the English Civil War, the Napoleonic Wars and both the First and the Second World Wars.

Pendennis was prepared as a winter quarters for Prince Charles, the future Charles II, from October 1645, and he spent several weeks there early in 1646, leaving in early March for safety on the Isles of Scilly. (His mother Queen Henrietta Maria had also stayed briefly in July 1644 before escaping to France.)

The Killigrews were an ancient and prominent Cornish family who lived at the manor of Arwenack in the lee of Pendennis. In the 1540s John Killigrew (d. 1567) was made the first governor of Pendennis Castle. His eldest son, also called John, succeeded as governor of the castle and, like his father and many other gentlemen seafarers of the day, colluded with the very pirates he was employed to challenge. His wife, Mary, seems to have taken part in her husband's activities. The Killigrews rebuilt their home, Arwenack, in 1567, incorporating defensive features such as gun ports.

When it comes to ghosts at Pendennis, there are many: a child visiting with his grandparents gave a detailed description of a soldier in the shell store of Half-Moon Battery; a former head custodian regularly saw a young woman on the stairs of the keep when he unlocked it in the mornings; but it seems that the one-time lieutenant governor of the castle, Captain Philip Melvill, puts in some of the most regular appearances. He was appointed in 1797 and remained at Pendennis until his death in 1811. At the age of nineteen he had been sent with his regiment to India where he was severely wounded, taken prisoner, and kept in brutal conditions for four years. His injuries, which were left untreated, never healed, and he was invalided out of active service. He liked to sit in his chair at the window of his rooms at Pendennis, watching the boats in the bay. Staff report that they frequently find a chair moved to this window in his old rooms on the first floor of the castle forebuilding. They also hear the sound of it being dragged there. And, as a member of staff points out – why dragged? Would Melvill not have lifted it? Melvill's old wounds from India meant that he had the use of only one arm; his left he wore in a sling.

Berry Pomeroy Castle, Devon

Tucked away in Devon woodland, Berry Pomeroy Castle must be counted among the most picturesque and romantic ruins in England. It has also built up a reputation as one of the most haunted. Built by the Pomeroy family in the fifteenth century during the Wars of the Roses, it was later acquired in the mid-sixteenth century by Edward Seymour, 'Protector Somerset' – the most powerful man in the realm – and was developed by the Seymour family into a great mansion, so ambitious and grandiose in scale that the money eventually ran out, and the site was abandoned by 1700.

While many of the ghost stories about the castle may be attributed to the imagination of the Victorians, there does seem to be something that troubles this place. It manifests itself chiefly in malfunctioning technology: failing cameras and smart phones, and inexplicable footage taken by a professional cameraman filming on site. He discovered the film to be entirely blank, though the audio track was intact, if disturbed by 'occasional screeches and other odd noises'. One visitor recalled driving here with his friends one night in his youth. They saw something white in the woods and ran back to their cars in terror – but none of their cars would start. They fled on foot and returned the next morning only to find that their cars started perfectly. It took twenty years before one of the men dared to return to the spot with his partner, but she ended up visiting the castle alone. There was no way, he said, he was going 'in there'.

Farleigh Hungerford Castle, Somerset

Sir Thomas Hungerford began this fortified mansion in the 1370s. It was extended by his son and remained in the Hungerford family until the late seventeenth century, when the notorious spendthrift Sir Edward Hungerford sold it. In the vault of the family chapel there is a unique collection of human-shaped lead coffins, the resting place of this somewhat scandal-plagued family. Two were executed during the Wars of the Roses. Another, who imprisoned his own wife at the castle for four years, half-starving her and attempting to poison her, was later beheaded beside Thomas Cromwell by Henry VIII, accused of treason, witchcraft and homosexuality. By this time he was considered by his contemporaries so 'unquiet' as to be mad.

But none of these Hungerford men are said to haunt the buildings, rather it is Lady Agnes Hungerford who is sometimes seen in the chapel – perhaps repenting her deeds. Agnes was convicted of inciting and abetting two of her servants to murder her first husband, after which his body was disposed of in the castle kitchen's oven and she promptly married Sir Edward Hungerford. After her second husband's death she and the servants were hanged at Tyburn.

Old Wardour Castle, Wiltshire

This remarkable castle in a remote valley was built by John, 5th Lord Lovell, one of the richest barons in England, in the 1390s. It was at the time as sophisticated as any building in Europe, its hexagonal design pioneering in its arrangement of luxurious self-contained suites for guests and its whole a symbol of Lovell's closeness to the opulent court of Richard II – a cousin of his wife. In 1578 the new owner, Sir Matthew Arundell, decided to modernise this exquisite castle, adapting it for Elizabethan living. But during the Civil War in the 1640s it was besieged, partially blown up, and afterwards left to fall into ruin.

The usual ghost at Old Wardour is said to be that of Sir Thomas Arundell's wife, the indomitable Lady Blanche, who in her husband's absence during the Civil War mustered twenty-five men and servants, and withstood a siege against 1,300 Parliamentarians for six days before surrendering. But what visitors report encountering on the spiral staircase is not the figure of brave Blanche but a light, as if of a lantern, and the sound of a deep groan.

Portland Castle, Dorset

This squat, compact coastal artillery fortress was built for Henry VIII in 1540 to protect the important anchorage known as the Portland Roads. It was one of a chain of such forts built along the southern coast at a period of threatened invasion from Catholic Europe. It remained armed and garrisoned into the nineteenth century, was then converted into a private house, but returned to military use at the end of the century and remained in service until after the Second World War. During the Civil War, the island of Portland was a Royalist stronghold, while the nearby merchant town of Weymouth backed Cromwell. The castle was much fought over, and taken and retaken several times by both Parliamentarian and Royalist forces.

Richard Wiseman, a Royalist surgeon, and later surgeon to Charles II, recalled attending to one of the soldiers of the Portland Garrison in 1645. The man was haemorrhaging, and Wiseman cauterised the wound, using a heated poker. As well as pushes and pinches in otherwise empty rooms, when in the castle kitchen, where this surgery is said to have taken place, visitors have reported the smell of burning flesh.

Yorkshire and the Humber

York Cold War Bunker, York

The Cold War Bunker in York, headquarters of the Royal Observer Corps, No. 20 Group, was opened in 1961 at the height of the Cold War. In 1949, the unstable relationship between the Soviet Union and the Western Allies following the Second World War deteriorated when the Soviets detonated a test nuclear bomb. In response Britain intensified its nuclear arms development and began to research and plan for possible nuclear attack. In 1956, the Ministry of Works began designs for nuclear-resistant bunkers. York Cold War Bunker was one of twenty-nine such bunkers built to form a network of semi-secret posts to observe and monitor nuclear attack. It was built underground of reinforced concrete, three storeys deep, 'tanked' in three layers of asphalt protected by brickwork, and then covered with earth. Here, after the world outside had been devastated and contaminated, a body of service men and women would seal themselves off behind the airlock doors and attempt, from the operations room at the heart of this sunken asylum, to make contact with the surviving outer world. The bunker remained manned and ready until it was decommissioned in 1991.

Perhaps due to its short and mercifully uneventful life – only thirty years, and witness only to peacetime activities – there are no known accounts of ghosts here. Instead this chilling underground stronghold seems to be haunted by its own once-dreaded fate.

Scarborough Castle, North Yorkshire

Scarborough Castle stands on a dramatic promontory with sweeping panoramic views over the North Sea and surrounding coastline. The Romans built a signal station here in the fourth century AD and Henry II's massive twelfth-century great tower still dominates the site. The castle was besieged several times, notably by rebel barons in 1312, and twice during the Civil War. It was shelled and badly damaged by German warships during the First World War.

It was during the siege of 1312 that the favourite of Edward II, Piers Gaveston, who had taken refuge in the castle, was captured. Although promised safe conduct on his surrender, he was seized on the return south by his great enemy the Earl of Warwick – whom Gaveston had disparagingly named the 'Black Dog' – and summarily beheaded. Visitors have reported being pushed and shoved in empty rooms, and, according to local legend, the ghost of Gaveston tries to lure people to their death over the edge of the castle cliff.

Whitby Abbey, North Yorkshire

The great ruins of the abbey can be seen from many miles away, dominating the headland above picturesque Whitby. The first abbey was founded here in 657 by King Oswiu of Northumbria, and its first abbess was the formidable Anglo-Saxon Princess Hild. It was here that the cowherd Caedmon was miraculously inspired to become a poet and the great synod of Whitby was held in 664 to determine the future direction of the Church in England. This abbey was abandoned in the ninth century, probably after Viking raids. The ruins seen today are not of this abbey but of the one founded in the eleventh century by a Benedictine monk, Reinfrid. The new abbey grew to be one of the most powerful monasteries in Yorkshire, but was suppressed in 1539. Part of it was converted into a handsome mansion, a section of which remains today. The Gothic ruins provide the unforgettable backdrop to the arrival of Dracula in England in Bram Stoker's novel. In his book, Lucy Westenra is curious about the ghost of a 'white lady' said to have been seen at one of the abbey's windows, though a sceptical local tells her bluntly that such stories are 'all very well for comers and trippers an' the like, but not for a nice young lady like you.'

Byland Abbey, North Yorkshire

The Cistercian abbey of Byland was regarded in its heyday as one of the three great abbeys of Yorkshire, alongside Rievaulx and Fountains. The enormous late twelfth-century church was bigger than most cathedrals of the time. Its west front, which dominates the ruins with the remains of a great circular rose window above three tall pointed lancet windows, proclaims Byland as an outstanding example of early Gothic architecture, a pioneer of the style in northern England. At the Suppression, Byland passed into private ownership, and fell into ruin. But one of the most remarkable survivals from the abbey is the medieval collection of ghost stories written in Latin by one of the monks at Byland in about 1400. One of the strangest tales clearly troubled the writer so much that he expresses the hope that he may not come to any harm for having written it down. It relates how, in days gone by, Jacob Tankerlay, a former rector of a nearby parish, who had been buried in front of the monks' chapter house at Byland, would rise from his grave at night to visit his former mistress. One night he 'breathed out into her eye'. It is not clear exactly what this means but the verb *exsufflare* (literally, 'to blow out') is used in the context of exorcism at baptism and also associated with magic rites. Whatever happened, the consequence was that the abbot and chapter took the drastic step of excavating the coffin and having it thrown into a lake. The monk concludes by praying that God should have mercy on Jacob if he is among the souls to receive salvation.

Helmsley Castle, North Yorkshire

The ruins of Helmsley Castle stand on a rocky outcrop above the River Rye. It was first built in the early twelfth century by Walter Espec, a Norman baron of 'gigantic stature' with a voice 'like a trumpet', known for his soldiering and his piety – he founded nearby Rievaulx Abbey and Kirkham Priory. Helmsley passed to his sister's husband, Peter de Ros, and he and his descendants raised most of the massive stonework defences seen today. In 1508, Helmsley came into the hands of Thomas Manners, who remodelled part of the castle into a luxurious mansion. The castle's only – but significant – military trial was a siege in 1644 during the Civil War. It was held by a small garrison for the king for three months before surrendering, during which time four men were killed. Later in the Civil War, Royalist prisoners were held in the basement of the west tower. It is one of these unhappy soldiers, killed by cannon fire or simply returning to the place of a wretched imprisonment, who is said to be seen sitting among the castle ruins.

The East of England

Audley End, Essex

This magnificent Jacobean house was built on the site of Walden Abbey, a twelfth-century Benedictine monastery that was suppressed on 22 March 1538. Five days later Henry VIII gave it to his Chancellor, Thomas, Lord Audley, to adapt for his own use. Audley converted the ranges around the monks' cloister into a courtyard house. He demolished the east end of the church, which extended from the north side of the cloister into what is now the parterre, or formal garden. Its foundations, as well as burials in what would have been the monks' cemetery, were discovered during work on this garden. Audley's grandson, Thomas Howard, Earl of Suffolk, rebuilt the house between 1605 and 1614 on a palatial scale. Charles II bought this ready-made palace from the 3rd Earl in 1667; then Audley End was returned to the Howards in 1701. Later in the century the Countess of Portsmouth began remodelling the house and gardens. She bequeathed it to her nephew in 1762, who commissioned Lancelot 'Capability' Brown to transform the gardens and Robert Adam to add a fashionable suite of reception rooms. In the 1820s, the 3rd Baron Braybrooke, a scholar and antiquarian, redecorated many of its rooms in the Jacobean style.

The massive oak screen in the great hall, with its carved busts and festoons of fruit, was probably originally brightly painted. In the eighteenth century it was painted white to represent the then fashionable stucco. The 3rd Baron stripped the screen back to the wood, as it remains today, and bought Jacobean furniture and an eclectic collection of arms to display in the house. His son, the 4th Baron, had a passion for natural history and his collection of stuffed and mounted animals is to be seen in the house.

There is no known curse attached to the screen, as in Sarah Perry's story, nor a monk who hanged himself here, but staff have experienced various peculiar happenings. A couple of years ago after closing time two members of staff doing a final check in the great hall smelt violets before the portrait of Margaret Audley. They summoned a colleague, who smelt the same thing. The scent moved about the hall and then simply vanished. On another occasion, a staff member was standing at the window outside the chapel when she felt the presence of someone behind her. She turned to see a tall aristocratic-looking man in dark clothing who then walked into the chapel. She followed him, but he had vanished. A black and white dog was seen in the butler's pantry by a new member of staff showing visitors round. She assumed it was a guide dog only to discover there were no dogs in the building. Oddly, Lord Howard de Walden and his wife, who rented Audley from 1904, left in 1912 after becoming convinced the place was haunted: while playing billiards he had seen a dog 'rush in through the wall'.

Bury St Edmunds Abbey, Suffolk

The abbey, founded in 1020, became one of the richest and most powerful Benedictine monasteries in England. The surviving structures are extensive and include the impressive Great Gate and remains of the immense church and monastic complex. The site became home to the remains of Edmund, king of the East Angles (d. 869), in 903 and the acquisition of such a notable relic made the monastery a place of pilgrimage as well as the recipient of numerous royal grants. It was here in 1214 that King John's discontented barons assembled to discuss their grievances against him – which led to Runnymede and the sealing of Magna Carta the following year. Although after the Suppression the abbey precinct was soon stripped of valuable building material, the abbot's lodging survived as a house until 1720.

Bury's monks must have been deeply attached to the abbey. Sightings of monastic ghosts are numerous and wide ranging. In the 1960s Enid Crossley, who lived in a cottage built in the medieval remains of the abbey, claimed that a monk regularly crossed her bedroom. Another has been seen disappearing through the wall of a butcher's shop and hanging around the basement of a local pub. He may be the lover of the spectral nun in grey, said to have been involved with one of the monks of Bury, and often seen around the place – occasionally in the pub.

Castle Rising Castle, Norfolk

This spectacular keep, one of the best preserved and most lavishly decorated in England, stands with its associated buildings surrounded by massive earthworks on a broad spur above the village of Castle Rising. Norman lord William d'Albini began work on the castle in 1138 for his new wife, the widow of Henry I. In the fourteenth century it became the luxurious residence of Queen Isabella, widow of Edward II, and the suite of buildings to the south of the keep was probably built for her. After her death it was held by the Black Prince, who ordered and authorised various building works here. In 1544 it was granted by Henry VIII to the Howard family in whose hands it remains today; the current owner is also a descendant of d'Albini, the castle's founder.

It is the presence of the formidable Isabella which is felt most strongly at Castle Rising, where visitors believe they have heard the skirts of her dress rustling on the stairs and in the white room, one of the upper chambers of the castle. In 2015, during an investigation, a photograph was taken in this room that revealed an unexpected shape: the shadowy figure of a woman in medieval dress.

Framlingham Castle, Suffolk

Framlingham is a magnificent late twelfth-century castle, its striking outline reflected in its glassy mere. The castle was built by Roger Bigod, Earl of Norfolk, one of the most influential courtiers under the Plantagenet kings. It remained the home to the earls and dukes of Norfolk for over 400 years, after which it was briefly owned by Mary Tudor, where she mustered her supporters in 1553 after the death of her brother, Edward VI. At the end of the sixteenth century, by now partly ruinous, the castle was used as a prison to hold Catholic priests and recusants. In about 1600 it held forty prisoners. The following century a poorhouse was built within its walls. It was occupied until 1839.

As to ghosts, staff at Framlingham report footsteps in the upper room of the medieval hall that now forms the Lanman Museum, as well as 'constant muttering' on the back stairs. One winter evening while alone in the castle, a member of staff heard a bell ring right beside her – the sort of hand bell that might have been used in the poorhouse to summon the inmates. On another occasion, one of the stewards arrived at the castle one morning and, as she went to turn on the lights, she saw a man standing dressed all in black wearing a Puritan-style hat and long cloak. She has never seen him again – fortunately – as she vows she would no longer be working at the castle if she had.

The Midlands

Kenilworth Castle, Warwickshire

Situated in the heart of England, Kenilworth was one of the mightiest fortresses in the country, a vast castle which withstood a famous medieval siege and is renowned for its association with Elizabeth I and her favourite, Robert Dudley, the Earl of Leicester, to whom the queen granted the castle in 1563. A castle was first established here in the 1120s. Later in the century Henry II took it under his control and it was his building work and that of his son, King John, that extended the castle to much the form it retains today. In 1244 this strategic and magnificent stronghold was granted by Henry III to Simon de Montfort – then a great royal favourite who strengthened the castle further and installed 'unheard of . . . machines' – probably the trebuchets (huge counterweighted catapults) that would soon to be used here in the longest medieval siege on English soil.

After the death of de Montfort during the Second Barons' War, his followers withdrew inside the castle. The king sent a messenger to demand their surrender. Instead, they sent him back to his master with a severed hand. The resultant great siege lasted six months. Disease and starvation finally forced the surrender of the rebels.

Kenilworth was subsequently developed as a palace by John of Gaunt, and became a favoured residence of the Lancastrian kings before passing to the Dudley family under Henry VIII. The last great works at the castle were carried out by Robert Dudley, Earl of Leicester, who built what is now known as Leicester's Building, a four-storey tower block erected in 1571 specifically to provide private accommodation for Elizabeth I. The queen visited four times, the last time in 1575, and the current Elizabethan gardens are a recreation of those Leicester created for that visit as part of his extensive efforts to impress the queen and win her hand in marriage.

The three-storey gatehouse in Kamila Shamsie's story was built by Leicester between 1570 and 1575. In 1650 it was converted into a house and an extension created at the back, where the staff office and kitchen now are. Staff have reported peculiar happenings in the gatehouse – things missing or moved once the castle has been closed to visitors, and the antique cot in the adjoining room rocking by itself. A night watchman reported that, while patrolling the grounds one evening, he witnessed a ghostly figure walk through his colleague, who went cold as it happened. Certainly, staff are used to various unexplained happenings. Some say ghostly chickens have even been seen pecking about the stables.

Bolsover Castle, Derbyshire

This extraordinary seventeenth-century aristocratic retreat stands on the site of a medieval castle perched high on a ridge above the Vale of Scarsdale. The medieval ruins were used as the setting for the exquisite Little Castle, built by Charles Cavendish from 1612 as an escape from his principal seat nearby. His son, William, added the terrace and the riding house, which remains the earliest complete survival in England. Charles I and Queen Henrietta Maria were entertained at Bolsover by Cavendish in 1634 with a lavish feast and entertainment. This was its heyday. By the end of the century the castle began to decline, though Cavendish descendants used it as a retreat until the early nineteenth century. Indeed, it remains occupied today, permanently it would seem.

Bolsover is one of the most widely reported haunted sites in the care of English Heritage. Members of staff and visitors often report being pushed, having doors slammed on them and finding objects inexplicably moved. Night security guards have been alarmed by unexplained lights and movement in the empty property, and two workmen were terrified when they saw a woman disappear through a wall. A little boy has been seen holding the hands of women or children as they walk about the site, his living companions unaware that he is at their side.

Hardwick Old Hall, Derbyshire

Hardwick Old Hall was built between 1587 and 1596 by Bess of Hardwick, who was among the richest and best-connected women of the Elizabethan age. The design was for the time radically modern, drawing on the latest Italian domestic innovations. Although now only a romantic shell, it suggests the magnificence of Bess's status and aspirations. When her fourth and final marriage, to George Talbot, 6th Earl of Shrewsbury, broke down acrimoniously, Bess retreated to Hardwick, where she enlarged and remodelled the medieval manor into the house now known as Hardwick Old Hall. When her husband died, leaving Bess staggeringly rich, she began work on a new hall immediately beside the old: the two intended to function like two wings of one building. Bess's descendants came to prefer Chatsworth to Hardwick, however, and in the eighteenth century the old hall was dismantled.

Staff and visitors alike have heard voices and non-existent doors opening and closing. It is said that the philosopher Thomas Hobbes, who enjoyed the patronage of the Cavendish family and died at Hardwick Hall in 1679, haunts the grounds. Here he is joined by Bess, who people claim still glides through her once magnificent creation.

Peveril Castle, Derbyshire

The 'Castle of the Peak', as Peveril was known in the Middle Ages, was founded soon after the Norman Conquest by the same powerful knight, William Peveril, who built Bolsover Castle. Its dramatic hilltop location high above what is now the Derbyshire town of Castleton was a clear position of dominance over the surrounding lands and it played an important role in guarding the Peak Forest lead-mining area. In 1155 it was taken into possession of the Crown, its defences strengthened and the keep built. The only real action that the castle saw occurred in 1216, at the end of the reign of King John. Despite the sealing of Magna Carter the year before, many of John's most powerful barons were still in rebellion, and Peveril was held for them by the constable of the Peak, Brian de Lisle. He was repeatedly ordered by the king to hand it over, refused, and was eventually ousted by force. How many of his or the king's men were killed at the time, if any, is not known, but reportedly a knight in a white surcoat has been seen standing beside the keep and on the ramparts, and a riderless horse and a black dog in the castle grounds – perhaps his? Visitors report banging and clanking, suggesting the iron-clad limbs of this same lonely knight still patrolling the castle walls.

After the death of John of Gaunt, who held the castle at the end of the fourteenth century, the castle fell into a decline from which it never recovered. Today it is one of the most romantic sites in this spectacular stretch of England.

Goodrich Castle, Herefordshire

Magnificent Goodrich stands in woodland on a rocky crag, commanding the valley of the River Wye. Goodrich led a largely peaceful existence until 1646, when Parliamentary forces under their commander Colonel John Birch bombarded and brought down the north-west tower before storming the castle and its Royalist garrison.

The keep was built in about 1150, probably by Richard 'Strongbow' de Clare and Goodrich subsequently passed to one of the greatest soldiers of that era, William Marshall, 'the best knight in all the world' according even to an enemy. But it was probably under William's granddaughter and her husband that the splendid castle whose remains dominate the site today was built. After its partial destruction in the Civil War the castle fell into ruin, a magnet for visitors in search of the Romantic and the Picturesque.

During the violent siege of Goodrich, so the story goes, Colonel Birch's niece, Alice, took refuge in the castle with her Royalist lover, Charles Clifford. As the battering of the castle by her uncle's men grew in violence, the lovers took fright and ran, trying to escape across the River Wye under cover of darkness. But the waters were high and they were swept away by the currents and drowned. They are said to be seen standing on the ramparts looking out across the valley.

The North West

Carlisle Castle, Cumbria

Carlisle Castle was built in 1092 by William II, in his efforts to secure the border between Scotland and England. His brother, Henry I, set about fortifying the castle in stone, but during the national crisis over the succession, David, king of the Scots, seized Carlisle, and shifted the Scottish border south again. He probably completed the works begun by Henry I at the castle and died there in 1135. But David's successor was no match for the next English king, Henry II, who regained and strengthened the castle, which was as well – twice the Scots attacked with large forces, and twice Carlisle withstood the sieges.

Under King John, Carlisle was again besieged by the Scots, who 'cracked from top to bottom' the walls of the outer gatehouse, and then surged inside and similarly bombarded the inner gatehouse. To the north of this inner gatehouse was the 'palace' – royal apartments where a bath was later installed for Edward I's queen, Margaret, who stayed at the castle while her husband was attempting to conquer Scotland.

In 1315 the Scots again attacked the castle, this time under Robert the Bruce, but the castle was staunchly defended under the command of Andrew Harclay, a then-favoured subject of Edward II. Some years later, however, Harclay attempted to negotiate a Scottish truce without the king's permission. The unfortunate man was surprised inside the castle, arrested for treason, and hanged, drawn and quartered outside the city walls. One of his quarters was displayed on Carlisle keep, where it remained for five years.

Carlisle was repeatedly strengthened during the rule of the Wardens of the March, the king's officers in charge of keeping the peace on the borders, but became neglected in the sixteenth century. But when Henry VIII's split with the Roman Catholic Church led to fears that the Scots, siding with Europe, would invade, Carlisle's importance was again recognised. Bulwarks were built to the east, the half-moon battery to the west, and the walls and roofs were strengthened to bear heavy guns. Carlisle gained some forty years' respite following the union of the crowns of England and Scotland in 1603, but when Civil War broke out those Scots who supported Parliament besieged the whole city, aiming to starve Carlisle into submission. Every horse was eaten, then the dogs, and finally the rats – and after nine months a desperate Carlisle surrendered.

During the Jacobite uprisings of 1715 and 1745, captured rebels were imprisoned in the city, including the castle. The prisoners taken after the defeat of the '45 uprising – during which Carlisle was once again besieged, this time by the Duke of Cumberland on his way north to victory at Culloden – did not fare as well as their fellows of '15. Then, two had escaped from the castle and the rest had been pardoned. But after the '45, although most were transported, thirty-one were hanged at Carlisle. Andrew Hurley refers to the drawing of lots by the prisoners to choose who would stand trial. This did indeed happen – the prisoners passing round a beaver hat in which were placed nineteen slips of white paper, and one of black. Nine unfortunate prisoners were executed at Carlisle on 18 October 1746. The event drew a large crowd but afterwards, 'many returned home with full resolution to see no more of the kind, it was so shocking'.

Carlisle remained a military base until 1959, during which time various works were done to extend and update the castle, including extensive new accommodation for troops. It seems to be one of these newer buildings, where the King's Own Border Regiment Museum is now housed, that has given rise to the most recent reports of oddities by staff, including alarms being set off, footsteps, banging doors and lights that have been turned off at night being on again in the morning.

Birdoswald Roman Fort, Cumbria

Lying within a meander of the River Irthing with a view into the gorge that was once compared to that of Troy, Birdoswald was one of the forts built by the Romans as part of the Hadrian's Wall frontier system. Its defences are the best preserved of any along the Wall. By the sixteenth century, Birdoswald was a fortified farm subject to raids by reivers from Liddesdale, now in Scotland. Birdoswald was farmed until 1984. Although there are rumours of a grey lady, the farmer's family who lived here between 1956 and 1984 never saw her – although that didn't prevent them from teasing the new hired hands, not to mention one or two archaeologists. One man was so scared after a picture fell off the wall one night that he left the next morning. The ghost was evidently more restless in earlier times, for the people who had lived at the farm previously heard chairs falling over in the night. They thought it was something to do with the statue of the goddess Fortuna, from the Roman bathhouse, that was once kept in a passageway. It is now in Tullie House Museum and Art Gallery, Carlisle.

The North East

Housesteads Roman Fort, Northumberland

Housesteads falls roughly midway along Hadrian's Wall, which was begun in about AD 122 and stretches for seventy-three miles, spanning the narrowest stretch of northern

England. Housesteads was garrisoned for most of its active life by the first cohort of Tungrians, a body of about 800 soldiers brought from the part of the Empire that is now eastern Belgium.

After the withdrawal of the Roman Empire from Britain in AD 410, the fort was largely abandoned until the sixteenth century, when a lawless community of thieving 'moss troopers' based themselves here, thriving in this dangerous borderland between Scotland and England.

The milecastle referred to in Kate Clanchy's story is known as milecastle 37. These small gated forts were built, as their name suggests, roughly every Roman mile along the length of the Wall. Between each were two towers, or turrets, from which soldiers patrolling the Wall could look out over the deep ditch north of the Wall and into barbarian territory. The forts were built to a roughly standard design – a large rectangle with rounded corners, the ramparts built of stone or turf, with a gate on each of the four sides and regular towers along the perimeter. At the centre of the fort was the headquarters building, which contained a strongroom, shrine, administrative buildings and assembly hall. Flanking the headquarters were the commanding officer's quarters and granaries, while the rest of the fort contained the barracks, workshops and storehouses.

At Housesteads, a town grew up outside the fort to the south. Many finds from this part of the site are housed in the museum. This was built in 1936 to the same footprint as one of the Roman town buildings, thought to have been an inn or shop, excavated earlier that decade. But the inn revealed something rather more than dropped dice and coins when excavated. Buried under the clay floor of the back room were two skeletons. One was that of a man, with the tip of a knife still in his ribs. The other, more fragmentary, was probably a woman. As Romans buried their dead outside the town, there is no doubt this was a murder. But it is not the ghosts of this unfortunate couple that have been seen along the Wall. Instead it seems the soldiers chose to return. Sceptics might imagine Roman re-enactors have been mistaken by imaginative visitors, but apparently not. One of the most common sightings is of a soldier in Roman armour at milecastle 42, some five miles west of Housesteads. The man is seen several metres up in the air, at the original level of the Wall.

Tynemouth Priory and Castle, Tyne and Wear

Commanding a superb defensive position on a headland overlooking the River Tyne, the ruins of Tynemouth Priory and Castle are now surrounded only by gravestones and seagulls. But for most of its 2,000-year history, the headland was inhabited by communities of monks and soldiers. A monastic community was established here in the eighth century but its buildings were destroyed during the Viking invasions of the ninth and tenth centuries. The medieval ruins visible today belong to Tynemouth Priory, founded in the late eleventh century and dedicated to St Oswine (d. 651) whose body was preserved here in a rich shrine. Although the monastery was suppressed in 1539 it seems that one monk never left the place and still wanders through the graveyard.

Because of its strategic value in protecting the mouth of the Tyne, the headland was fortified until the 1950s. It is not within the remains of the medieval gatehouse nor the gun batteries where the latest oddity occurred but in the disused coastal station, not normally open to the public. A theatre company at Tynemouth which put on a show one recent Hallowe'en discovered that a projector, which had been carefully set up and left in a locked room, had been turned on its side.

Prudhoe Castle, Northumberland

Mighty Prudhoe was built in the early twelfth century, on the site of an earlier Norman fortress, to defend a strategic crossing of the River Tyne against Scottish invaders. It was continuously occupied for over nine centuries. Prudhoe was originally the home of the Umfravilles, and withstood two sieges, before passing to the Percy family in 1398. In the early nineteenth century they built a Regency style manor house for their land agent within its walls.

While local legend talks of a grey lady who haunts the former moat and surrounding woods and a white horse that drifts silently round the courtyard, one former resident of Prudhoe, who lived with her mother in the east tower (without electricity or running water) in the 1950s, witnessed other more disturbing phenomena. First, there was the sound of chanting from the chapel and, more unexpectedly, of someone bouncing a ball rhythmically up and down the steps outside. There had been a young boy, they were told, who later became a priest and used to spend hours practising bouncing a ball up and down the steps . . . Another resident and her husband were often awakened by the sound of water being hurled with great force at the door – although there was no trace of it on investigation.

In the hallway was an enormous oak table. One night an incredible noise woke everyone up, as if there had been an explosion. The massive top lid of the table lay on the floor. It could not possibly just have slipped or been pushed – it took three men to put it back in place.

BIOGRAPHICAL NOTES

Kate Clanchy was born in Glasgow and is the author of *Meeting the English*, shortlisted for the Costa First Novel Award, and the much acclaimed memoir *Antigona and Me*. Her poetry has won her a wide audience as well as three Forward Prizes and a Somerset Maugham Award, among others. The title story from *The Not-Dead and The Saved* won the 2009 BBC National Short Story Award.

Stuart Evers' first book, *Ten Stories About Smoking*, won the London Book Award in 2011 and his highly acclaimed novel, *If This is Home*, followed in 2012. His most recent collection, *Your Father Sends His Love*, was shortlisted for the 2016 Edge Hill Short Story Prize. His work has appeared in three editions of the *Best British Short Stories* as well as *Granta*, *The White Review*, *Prospect* and on BBC Radio 4. Originally from the North West, he lives in London.

Mark Haddon is a writer and artist who has written fifteen books for children and won two BAFTAs. His bestselling novel, *The Curious Incident of the Dog in the Night-time*, was published simultaneously by Jonathan Cape and David Fickling in 2003. It won seventeen literary prizes, including the Whitbread Award. His poetry collection, *The Talking*

Horse and the Sad Girl and the Village Under the Sea, was published by Picador in 2005, his play *Polar Bears* was performed at the Donmar Warehouse in 2007 and his last novel, *The Red House*, was published by Jonathan Cape in 2012. His latest full-length book is *The Pier Falls*, a collection of stories. He lives in Oxford.

Andrew Michael Hurley has lived in Manchester and London, and is now based in Lancashire. His first novel, *The Loney*, was originally published by Tartarus Press, a tiny independent publisher based in Yorkshire, as a 300-copy limited-edition, before being republished by John Murray and going on to win the Costa Best First Novel Award and Book of the Year at the British Book Industry Awards in 2016. He is currently working on *Devil's Day*, to be published by John Murray in 2017.

Andrew Martin is the author of a dozen novels, including a series of nine thrillers set on the railways of Edwardian Britain, one of which, *The Somme Stations*, won the Crime Writers' Association Award for Historical Fiction in 2011. His latest novel, *Soot*, is set in York in 1799 and concerns the murder of a silhouette painter. He also writes and presents TV documentaries.

Sarah Perry was born in Essex. She has been the writer in residence at Gladstone's Library and the UNESCO World City of Literature Residence in Prague. Her first novel, *After*

Me Comes the Flood, was longlisted for the Guardian First Book Award and the Folio Prize, and won the East Anglian Book of the Year Award in 2014. *The Essex Serpent* was the Waterstones Book of the Year in 2016 and won the British Book Awards Fiction Book of the Year and Overall Book of the Year in 2017. It was also shortlisted for the Costa Novel Award and the Dylan Thomas Prize, and longlisted for the Walter Scott, Baileys and Wellcome Book Prizes. She lives in Norwich.

Max Porter is the author of the bestselling *Grief is the Thing with Feathers* (Faber & Faber, 2015), which won the International Dylan Thomas Prize, the Sunday Times PFD Young Writer of the Year Award and the Books Are My Bag Readers Award, and was shortlisted for the Guardian First Book Award and The Goldsmith's Prize. It has been translated into twenty-eight languages. Max lives in south London with his wife and three children.

Kamila Shamsie is the author of seven novels, most recently *Home Fire*. *Burnt Shadows* has been translated into more than twenty languages and was shortlisted for the Orange Prize for Fiction, and *A God in Every Stone* was shortlisted for the Bailey's Women's Prize for Fiction. Three of her other novels (*In the City by the Sea, Kartography, Broken Verses*) have received awards from the Pakistan Academy of Letters. A Fellow of the Royal Society of Literature, and one of *Granta*'s 'Best of Young British Novelists', she grew up in Karachi, and now lives in London.

Jeanette Winterson OBE was born in Manchester. Adopted by Pentecostal parents, she was raised to be a missionary. This did and didn't work out. Discovering early the power of books, she left home at sixteen to live in a Mini and get on with her education. After graduating from Oxford University she worked for a while in the theatre and published her first novel at twenty-five. *Oranges Are Not The Only Fruit* is based on her own upbringing but using herself as a fictional character. She scripted the novel into a BAFTA-winning BBC drama. Twenty-seven years later she revisited that material in the bestselling memoir *Why Be Happy When You Could Be Normal?* She has written ten novels for adults, as well as children's books, non-fiction and screenplays. She writes regularly for the *Guardian*. She lives in the Cotswolds in a wood and in London. She believes that art is for everyone and it is her mission to prove it.